A TALL TALE AND JOURNEY TO ANOTHER REALM

GARY ALEXANDER AZERIER

Cyberwit.net
HIG 45 Kaushambi Kunj, Kalindipuram
Allahabad - 211011 (U.P.) India
http://www.cyberwit.net
Tel: +(91) 9415091004
E-mail: info@cyberwit.net

Printed at VCORE LLP.

ACKNOWLEDGEMENT

I would be more than remiss if I did not note the assiduous dedication and long hours of proofing, retyping and correcting sustained by my wife Rose Ann. Loyalty hardly describes her efforts. She had better things to do but was relentlessly persistent. Lewis Carroll would be proud. I am as well, and chortle in my joy.

Gary Alexander Azerier

PREFACE

Jabberwocky is a "nonsense" poem from <u>Alice Through The Looking Glass</u> written by Lewis Carroll in which a young man is jarred from a rather pleasant afternoon (although there is ostensibly some consternation among the local parrots and turtles) and warned to heed an encroaching foe. The lad's mentor, the voice in the poem, persuades him to take up arms, seek out and destroy the formidable threat. It has been some time since the protege has had to assume an aggressive posture, but with some thought and proper armament he pursues and successfully defends against the nasty and belicose enemy. Upon his return he is welcomed by his paternal figure, who acknowledges the young man's heroic deed and cheeringly commends him. Once more all is right with the world, and the no longer endangered community is again ensconced in its peculiar, but comfortably familiar, ways.

This story, TIMEGYRE, is a contemporary translation of **Jabberwocky,** using lines from the poem (like looking through a looking glass) to move the story along. The word "gyre" is from the poem ("the slithy Toves did gyre and gimble in the wabe") and means to go around and around, as in gyroscope. Timegyre means a going around through time. The use of the lines from the poem throughout the story also serves another purpose as explained by Solly's mentor, Dr. Berg, at the end of the story. Solly's story and the stream of events in which he finds himself enmeshed, is so in rapport with, and parallel to, the hero and <u>his</u> story in **Jabberwocky** that the two come together and become intertwined. Solly is on a predestined path whose road can also be discerned weaving its way through the "nonsense" stanzas of **Jabberwocky.**

Jabberwocky has been called a "nonsense" poem. But although some of its words and concepts are inventions of Lewis Carroll, both the words and the poem have meaning, a message, and do convey a "sense". My intention is similar for my expanded upon and parallel "nonsense", TIMEGYRE.

'Twas Brillig'...

Contents

TIMOTHY

It was staggering and unusual, and the most unreal thing he had ever witnessed. Sol Learner's brilliant friend, Timothy Gillis, had simply, although it was, more than likely, otherwise, in bright daylight, only an arm's length away, with no forewarning...vanished! The two men had been conversing at a small table at the Conservatory Lake Cafe in Central Park when the unpredictable Timothy turned about in his chair, bent down as if to recover a dropped utensil...and, quite suddenly, vanished! There was not a trace of him. Timothy was nowhere in sight. And there seemed little doubt about the fact, or illusion...or whatever it was, Timothy had indeed exited the place, the day, the dimension, in a wholly unusual manner that apparently could not be explained according to convention. He was nowhere! And only a few hours earlier the two of them had stood, together, in the flesh, at the 72nd Street and 5th Avenue entrance to the park. Timothy had had something of importance to tell Solly. Now, stunned and alone, Solly, not without anxiety, compulsively recalled that conversation. Word for word.

"Listen, Solly, here's the way it is." Timothy tucked his large hands into his jacket pockets as the two men continued on their walk. The day was bright with sun. The park was lush with green.

"You see," he said, "one of the big questions people kept asking after World War II was" Timothy paused to relight his Meerschaum, "was how the Germans, coming right out of what was perhaps the most advanced civilization the world had ever known, could ever have been responsible for...perpetrated what were the most monstrous, utterly heinous, atrocities, imaginable. After all, Solly, how could such a people so advanced in music: Beethoven, Bach, Handel; in philosophy: Kant, Hegel, I dare not say Nietzsche; mathematics: Gauss, Leibniz; civilized organization; how could such a people attempt, no, conceive, then attempt, never mind succeed, how could they conceive of the systematic eradication of selected groups of people?" Solly made no attempt to answer as Timothy puffed leisurely on his pipe, trying to get it going once again. Timothy would not have entertained any answers in any case. He continued.

"Well, you see, Solly, that was not really the question. It was more the key. Because only such a civilized people could ever have seriously contemplated genocide...and could actually have taken it through the planning and, no pun, execution stages. It never could have occurred to a less advanced society. Certainly, it never could have been borne out on such an immense scale. The perverted idea of a racial purity coupled with the enormity of genocide, the assassination of an entire people, could only have occurred to the Germans because, you see, they had the complete capability of carrying it out through their highly sophisticated system of filing, record keeping, and data processing. From there, organization and enforcement was easy. But it was in fact these stores of records and data that brought this complex system of perverted concepts initially to the mind of the collective Teutonic instigating body." Solly's mind had begun to wander when he noticed the two shadowy figures evenly pacing themselves a few steps behind Timothy and himself. He noticed them because he thought he had seen them before, although he could not quite recall when. Solly stopped and looked about, as if simply taking in the afternoon air and freshness. The two men behind also stopped. Timothy, quite content to carry on while standing still, continued.

"Those very facts and files on everyone in the bloody country taking up so much room, maintenance, time and effort, cried out to be put to use. For purposes good...or purposes evil." He began a casual step again, reaming his pipe, which had begun burning nothing more than a smoldering bit of ash at the bottom of the bowl. The two men Solly had noticed started walking also.

"The Germans," Timothy continued, "could not economically afford to utilize these confidential documents for anything beneficial. After all, how could they be used to bring about anything productive? Destructive would be more inherent in the nature of such material. And, the files, comprehensive as they were, made personal invasions, control and enforcement, for purposes of evil, all too facile. The irony, Solly, is that only a society having reached the very heights of organizational capability could have conceived such notions. But...once the possibilities clearly presented themselves and showed they could be carried out with dispatch and relative facility, with only a little encouragement and, shall we say, rabble rousing, the choice became unavoidable." A light breeze came out of the West and Solly felt it especially about his neck. He raised his jacket collar. The new wind did not seem to have any effect on Timothy.

He barely paused at all. "At first," he went on, it was to try an experiment. Just to see. Of course it will be tried. Then, the curiosity, the experiment, becomes a compulsion, an obsession, a frenzy! Like the appetite of a big cat after his first taste of raw meat." Solly slowly and very carefully turned around. The two men were nowhere to be seen. Timothy was restuffing his pipe. Tamping it. Lighting it. He eyed the flame as part of it was being sucked into the bowl. Slowly he said, "We are just beginning to understand what it was the Germans did and how they went about doing it...because, Solly, we ourselves are becoming capable of doing the very same thing! And Solly, certain factions, very important factions, very high up, are beginning to take themselves very seriously." He drew the words out. "Very seriously".

Solly fidgeted, rubbed his face, and appeared uncomfortable with the last point Timothy had been trying to make. It was late, they had been walking for some time now, it was growing a bit chilly, and besides, Solly was getting hungry. When Timothy got into one of his philosophical moods he could ramble on for hours but, Solly thought, there was something slightly different about this little session. Timothy had called him out this afternoon, especially to talk to him about something specific. And now he seemed to be getting down to cases. Still, Solly felt compelled to interrupt.

"Are you telling me...we might do...or are capable of doing what the Nazis did in Germany in the 30's and 40's? I mean, is that even possible?"

"Not just possible, Sol, it is going to happen!" Timothy took the moment to relight his pipe, as if for added effect. "It's just a question of time. We weren't capable before, now we are. We have the expertise to make it happen. Now we are the expert file clerks, record keepers and data managers. And always remember when something can happen, slick and easily, with a minimum of effort, visibility and time, it eventually will happen. Unless..." Solly jumped on the word.

"Unless what?"

"I'll tell you in a moment. But first, Solly, let me make clear what is about to happen, and why. Just imagine those who direct our society. I'm not talking necessarily about those in government. More, let us say, those behind government. Imagine them as being hobbyists. Their work is their hobby... and their entire life. It is their <u>sole</u> obsession. Now you really do have to imagine this because it is not the way most people conduct their affairs. Occupation for these men is an entirely different pursuit. It is a quest for something more than mere power. It is an all encompassing hobby, an inordinate, consuming passion, and, in order to achieve his goals, the hobbyist will stop at virtually nothing. The fact that these goals may be irrational or even twisted is not apparent, much less meaningful, to him. If he possesses the means of achieving his ends he shall use these means despite who stands in the way or who must be sacrificed. The hobby comes first".

As the path they were on drew to an end, a clearing up ahead came into view, and somehow Solly felt the afternoon sinking. His stomach seemed to follow. He had become aware that some of his thoughts had been wandering. His attention had drifted to nowhere in particular for some moments during Timothy's talk, and now he was faced with the rather formidable task of making sense out of what his friend was earnestly trying to convey. In the clearing now Solly could make out the backs of the magnificient Mad Hatter, Alice and the Hare, pocket watch in hand, in the midst of their tea party.

"I'm not altogether sure I quite get what you're driving at, Tim. I mean, what do...hobbies have to do with...?"

Timothy took Solly's sleeve and gently tugged him to a halt. "Just so you'll understand. Let's draw one side of our analogy by examining a hobby. What one generally does in a hobby of say...collecting, because these men are essentially collectors, is to spend time cataloging and classifying, numbering and assessing. That is, putting values on what lies at the heart of the hobby: stamps, coins, art objects, antiques, paintings. This is part of the hobby. Then, before seeking out new pieces, there is the trimming and editing of the collection. Weeding out, constantly upgrading, replacing, restocking. And the constant sorting: changing places and configurations, separating, joining, making more space, consolidating, making room for the new, getting rid of the old. Inbetween this ongoing regrouping and sorting and the pursuit to acquire new and rare pieces, the collector is always ready to show, display and exhibit his col

"No, Solly. That's just the point. It does not matter if one's passion is tennis or gambling, or collectibles, or books or magic. Unless the hobbyist's end is merely to fritter away time, and that is hardly a hobby, he is concerned with the equip-ment necessary to maintain his hobby, a certain...shall we say, preparation ritual, sorting, cataloging and classifying. It all falls under the heading of collecting. That's a major point. And, here's another. Each collection grows...in one direction or another."

The two of them walked through the Tea Party and down the few steps towards the Conservatory Lake. Solly looked at his watch. It <u>was</u>

late. Fourthirty p.m. to be precise. Just a little after brillig, he mused. *'Twas brillig, and the slithy toves did gyre and gimble in the wabe...'*

It isn't easy to take a casual glance at one's watch when someone is issuing forth some rather lengthy discourse.

Timothy did not provide for any exception to this. "Well," he emphatically voiced, "we're getting around to a pivotal factor here. Everything always comes down to taking hold of that most rare item. That elusive,long forgotten story, that most difficult opponent, the long sought after win, the well deserved triumph, that delicate skill, rare trophy. The impossible dream. We are talking about the rare, hidden, elusive, costly, delicate, long lost, oddsagainst, nearly nonexistent, experience of experiences. And that, is what collecting is really all about. It is a stepladder to the unreachable...without the arduous climbing of which, the unreachable would be unappreciated."

Timothy had a marvelous passion that embraced his words when he spoke. But, at times, it could almost embarrass the less dramatic spirit. Solly felt compelled to temper Timothy's fervor.

"So I'll start chasing butterflies. What has all this to do with government?"

"Let's go over there," Timothy gestured to the little cake house across the boat basin, "I want to get something to drink. Hungry?"

The two of them walked around the water to the pleasant sunlit area of chairs, tables and umbrellas and the green and white sign that said REFRESHMENTS. And that in itself was, in a way, refreshing.

"You see," said Timothy, followed by a long draw on his Diet Cola, "most men are collectors. Some men collect stamps, some collect fine art. I've known men who collected cars. A friend of mine collected lots. Real estate lots. Never developed them or built on them. Just collected them. Some men collect stocks and bonds, or gold certificates. They don't buy and sell, mind you. That's different. They just collect.

Men can collect anything from pieces of barbed wire to publishing companies, from unique variations of items in a given class to repeated examples of the item over and over again. I knew a gentleman once who collected black cast iron hoot owls. They had to be black hoot owls, and they had to be cast iron. He had hundreds of them. Somewhere in the back of his mind he probably entertained the notion that someday he would own every last black cast iron hoot owl in the world. Then where would the world be?"

"But suppose," Solly interrupted, "suppose there were no such owls to be found? Suppose your friend were stranded on a desert island?"

"First, if there were no owls to be found, hc would be apt to search harder. He would become more passionate, more driven, and eventually, more frustrated. Eventually his lust for owls would become sublimated. Displaced. Rechanneled. If he were on a desert island, he would begin collecting seashells." Timothy took a long look around and seemed uncomfortable to Solly. "Of course, this wouldn't work especially well on a desert island, but some men have been known to collect women...or wives. Trophies, so to speak. Henry the Eighth was one such man, although it might be argued his preference was more accurately for women's heads. Remember Tommy Manville? Mickey Rooney? You might say they were collecting. It was their hobby. It's all the same passion. The same lust. The same obsession. It is only the object that changes. What you have to keep in mind is the more rare, the more exotic, the greater the danger and risk, the more outrageous...the more attractive the object of desire. Sometimes however, I must add, the collector and his fever are taken by surprise. The hobby, the collection, was not planned. As in the case of our Government friends, they are eased into the game. Just like an unsuspecting pot smoker who tries crack for the first time suddenly finds...a short while later, he's hooked."

Solly stood up. "I'll get us some coffee. Be right back." Solly had had a recent history of long walks and talks with Timothy, after the monthly meetings of **QUARK,** that strange and esoteric offshoot of its parent club to which they both belonged, **MENSA.** And had it not been for what he knew of the philosophical Timothy, the hints of mysticism and odd speculations that the brooding thinker would casually, but persistently and regularly drop, had it not been for a strange aura of the unusual and preternatural in which Timothy seemed to exist, Solly would not have known what to think. But Timothy <u>had</u> had some of the strangest and most exotic tales to tell, of the most unlikely connections, and he had posed some of the most implausible possibilities from time to time...that Solly had, more or less, been expecting...well, he didn't quite know exactly <u>what</u> he had been expecting. But the uneasy feeling had been with him for some days now.

As Solly sauntered over toward the refreshment stand he failed to notice the two men in gray suits and neckties on either side of the food counter. They both looked down as Solly approached. Timothy had noticed them when they first sat down.

Solly carefully placed the two coffees on the table so as not to spill anything. "So...you were saying?"

Timothy leaned in toward Solly. He spoke in nearly a whisper. "The men in power now are very powerful. More than ever. There is nothing they want for. Virtually everything is at their disposal. Their funds are unlimited. They have round the clock staffs. Beck and call transportation to and from anywhere. They have immunity from any legal or bureaucratic hassles or entanglements. Any women...any time. Now I ask you....What else is there? The hobby. That's what else. They own you. You...and me...and everyone else. You see, Solly, they collect us. <u>We're</u> the hobby. And they have us numbered, named and classified. We have been assessed, evaluated and ranked. We are duly filed in the computer. We can be called up, located, and dealt with anytime and in any way they choose. They make the rules and they can change the rules. We can be edited, trimmed, even weeded out. We can be replaced...even upgraded. Soon, in fact, they will be capable of rapidly instituting any changes they like or deem necessary. But not just yet.

You see, right now, they just don't want us to make too many changes. At this point we still enjoy the illusion of a free society, but, you may notice, even the illusion is being eroded." Timothy paused long enough to let what he had just said sink in. "What we're really entertaining is more or less an echo, an after image, of what we once knew of our free society...what sleight of hand magicians like to call a **retention pass.** You really think you see the coin, but you don't. What you retain...is the <u>image,</u> or after image, of the coin...as the coin <u>itself</u> is stolen away. We retain the <u>image</u> of our freedom, as freedom <u>itself</u> is covertly stolen away from us. But soon, there won't even be the illusion. In the meantime they're just watching us." Had Solly been swallowing his mouthful of coffee at the moment, all within earshot could have heard him gulp. But, as was the case, he just sat there with his mouthful. What Timothy had said was difficult enough to swallow. Besides, Solly felt as if he did not want to make a sound. Perhaps it was to avoid calling any unnecessary attention to himself.

"Our society," Timothy continued undaunted, "is currently capable of the most rapid and advanced methods of calculating, computing and sorting. Matching, batching and resorting. We are capable," he smiled a little cynical smile, "of filing, compiling, collating and locating. And you Solly, you and I, arc no more than a keystroke away from delete." Solly finally let the coffee go down. But it didn't go easily. "The Germans were the greatest and most efficient record keepers and file clerks of all time. Fanatic about it, you might say. And they finally put it to use. Well we have a more awesome capability now. And we too will put it to use. A use, I'm afraid," said Timothy, "that will make the Teutonic atrocities seem like a Broadway musical. Our country, with all its ethnic minorities and diverse nationalities, will be steeped in a blood bath the likes of which the world, in all its butchering history, has never quite known. And that's saying something Solly." Timothy took out his Meerschaum again and stuffed it to the top. He struck a match and began drawing the flame in through the bowl. "But, you know something, Solly," Timothy said as he puffed some of the acrid Latakia across the table, "Americans don't like to be collectibles in some twit's hobby. They just won't buy it when the truth becomes plain." Another series of puffs. "Unfortunately, that's going to take **some** time. I know. I've been there. With those two." Timothy gestured with a slight movement of his head. Then he looked up and smiled in the direction of the two men sipping SevenUps a few feet away. They offered no expressions in return. Their faces were as close to blanks as you could draw. Timothy turned back and addressed Solly sternly. "See", he said, "I've already seen it happen, Solly. Now this run is up to you." Timothy turned around in his chair once again, as if about to bend down to recover a dropped utensil,...and quite suddenly, he was gone. Vanished. Not a trace. The two men were gone also.

It was when Solly glared in amazement at the empty wrought iron chair across from where he was sitting that he saw it. There, after all, was a trace! It was a small leather notebook resting innocently next to Timothy's unfinished coffee. He reached for it, held it for a moment as he peered around once more, then carefully placed it in his jacket pocket, stood up and left.

DR. BERG

It was difficult to tell in the rain whether the cobblestones were brown or black. Or were they a little of each, highlighted occasionally by the flecks of color that materialize off wet rust? Perhaps it really depended on just how they caught the rain...and the light...and of course your eye. All color depended on that. If there were no light, and no reflection, and certainly if there were no viewer the stones would be...perfectly black. In fact, they might not even <u>be!</u> But that, thought Solly, was another story. Right now the rain was also making it very difficult to see the number on the building across the flickering cobblestone street. What difference would that make, Solly muttered to himself? He had momentarily forgotten the address he was looking for; the one in Timothy's leather notebook inside his raincoat, but he didn't want to risk getting the book wet. The bits of information inside were too important to be drizzled into Rorschachs. Not tonight anyway. Not before seeing Dr. Berg.

He dashed across the street to the curb and ducked underneath the stone arch before the black iron grille and glass door. Out of a smashedin pack, Solly took out an Old Gold regular, nonfilter cigarette, lit it, and took a couple of puffs as he tried to get the sense of who and where he was...and what he was trying to do.

'So rested he by a tumtum tree...and stood awhile in thought.'

Comforted by the quiet and his solitude he carefully drew out the notebook and opened it to the first page. **'Dr. Berg'** it said, **'320 Leroy, near Mercer, around corner from Bedford.** 'Then it said **'Hard to find. Inbetween two incorrectly sequenced numbers. Find black door of Mortimer's first. Go in. Have an ale then leave through the back court. Apt. 4J. Berg will explain. Tell Berg, Timothy had to travel again.'**

It wasn't very long before Solly found himself standing before Dr. Berg's door. It was black with a brass knocker held between lion's teeth. Two knocks brought a stout tweedy little man to the door. "Timothy," Solly cleared his throat....

"Is traveling again," finished Dr. Berg. "We've been expecting you. Come in and please sit down."

The room was spare and dimly lit by two little lamps on either side of a long, lace draped table against the side wall. In the center of the gray toned room were four chairs on which sat four young men.

"Draw up a chair and get comfortable," said. Dr. Berg as he himself straddled his bridge chair, its back facing the small group. "This is Dave, that's Bullets, the gentleman in the white turtleneck is Tough Tommy Dweyer, and last but not least is Peanuts, all euphonious appellations bestowed upon them by the inimitable proprietors of the Rackets, a grog dispensing Public House downstairs, and beyond reproach. Now, before some of us repair to that good establishment for an evening's lubrication, Solly, there are one or two more points I should like to embellish upon. And, oh yes everybody, this is Solly, soon to be dubbed with some more distinctive nomenclature by our erstwhile friends down at the Rackets." Dr. Berg, who had never mentioned <u>his</u> alias, leaned forward.

"All this stuff about going back and forth through time of course is a lot of nonsense." As he spoke he reached into his jacket pocket and removed a dark cherry Bjarne pipe. He tamped it down a bit and then proceeded to light it as he continued. "Because events," he puffed a cloud of sweet smelling smoke, "<u>events</u> do not linger along points in <u>space.</u> This nonlingering is one of the major characteristics which comprises the rather distinct nature of time. Back and forth, on the other hand, describes such lingering along points in space. Events in <u>time</u> are patterned bits of energy. The energy itself, its effect and its evolved forms, continues to exist but it is just not accessible along any back and forth <u>space</u> route. However, gentlemen, as sure as we can hear a tape, view a film, or catch the scent of that someone lovely who just passed by, we can look in again on any event that has ever occurred...here, there, or along any array of points on our space continuum. But <u>the event must have originally occurred at that point in space!</u> It would simply be a question of enhancement. Tuning and enhancement." Whenever Dr. Berg paused there was considerable stillness and silence as if the pause were needed not to interrupt or ask questions but to digest and absorb. "I know what some of you must be thinking," said Dr. Berg, "What about <u>future</u> events? Let me assure you this includes so called future events. You see, future events have already occurred. It's just that they occurred in the future. It's all relative. After all, you must realize, our future is someone else's past."

"But professor," interrupted the young man called Dave in his gray tweed jacket making the best of a well worn and slightly soiled oxford shirt beneath it, "what about the possibility of those events taking shape or reforming if you will, and impinging upon us now? I mean, instead of a one time, static, or rigid event, is there a possibility of a pattern of events or occurrences, or a pattern within events or occurrences, crashing through a time or space barrier and materializing for our perceptions...or even being recorded on a piece of electromagnetic tape, or film, or reflective surface, or what have you? And," Dave raised his finger as if to signal the real essence of his question, "could such an event repeat itself, or occur somewhere <u>prior</u> to its happening in real time?"

Dr. Berg stood up and lowered his pipe. "First of all we must get rid of this notion of 'real time' or 'real space'. There coexist many different levels of events: There are events which do not coexist with other event levels but which do nonetheless exist. In any case, certain events can, because of their nature and position, impinge themselves upon us. Let me try to explain. **When there is an earth shattering event of such momentum that the very fabric of time and space is shaken, its threads begin to come undone. The very force holding the weave**

together is jarred and its patterns start to come apart. The natural sequence of places and events, as we know them to occur, and as we know them to have occurred, is changed, however slightly, and begins to present a different face to us. Now, initially, this earth shattering event,let us call it a plosion, being neither an explosion nor an implosion, and happening either in the past or in the future, or even in the present, in order to have any effect on events or our perception of them, has to occur or have occurred within a certain vicinity of time and space and also must have inherent in it a specific bearing on the person whose life, or whose time and space fabric it effects.

What I'm talking about now," Dr. Berg continued, "can be likened to a strong wind blowing from someone's future...or even past for that matter."

"Analogy, Dr. Berg. Please!" called one of the young men. Solly had been listening too intently to notice who it was.

"Fine. But first allow me to try to describe this 'Earth shattering' event to which I referred a moment ago. Events, in themselves, simply consist of physical <u>disturbances</u>. Of course these disturbances do not have to be very great. They are just movements, of one set of molecules or atoms or particles or perceptions upon another set. This second set, incidentally, could be active or passive, even dormant. None of the particles is destroyed in the process. Only their patterns are altered. And, as I suggested earlier, by recapturing a set of particles and recreating the patterns to which they once belonged, and by doing so at a specific set of coordinates along the TSE or the timespaceexistence grid, events and their directions, origins, destinations, consequences and appearance can be recreated, even slightly altered." There was a bit of a gleam in Berg's eye. "Simple and fragmented examples of this would be the recording of sound, the taking of pictures and so on. The difference is in these examples only patterns are being recorded and not the <u>actual particles</u> involved in the event. <u>The actual particles still exist, however.</u> And their effects can again, at some future time be recorded. Now <u>if</u>

the particles remain in the same pattern, or if they can be rearranged to recreate <u>that same pattern, the very same event will reoccur!</u> But," and here Dr. Berg threw up his hands, "and I know all of you have been waiting for that recurring, ubiquitous 'but'...there are simply too many uncontrollable factors in our world that can, and do, determine pattern changes. Still, there are ways around this. And we were talking about Earth shattering events and future winds, impinging particles and altering tides, were we not? Remember Dave had asked a question about whether an event could crash through a time space barrier and reform, or materialize for our perceptions? Let me illustrate with an incident that recently happened to a friend of mine." Dr. Berg paused for a long deep breath and to undo two of the lower buttons on his vest which his stout frame appeared to have outgrown. No one in the room seemed to have noticed as all eyes were on the Doctor's face.

"My friend," continued Dr. Berg, breathing a bit easier, "had had an especially vivid dream that was both frightening and, in the end, a relief to him. He dreamed he was holding a revolver as it exploded in his hand. At first he was traumatized and petrified for fear that his hand and fingers were irreparably damaged. Slowly he tried moving his fingers and slowly they responded. By some miracle they were not affected by the blast. He awoke from his dream greatly relieved and incredulously moving his fingers. Moments later, while drying his hair with a hotcomb, the device crackled and then exploded...in his hand. Somehow, perhaps because of his prescient dream, my friend let the thing go just at the right moment. And on moving his fingers slowly, he discovered, much to his assurance, that although they were slightly singed from the blast, his digits suffered no damage other than that. It was the same sense of relief he had experienced in the dream."

"If it was not just coincidence, how would <u>you</u> explain the connection, Dr. Berg?" asked Bullets.

"Somehow the impact of this blast," continued Dr. Berg through a bit more smoke, "in what Dave would have called 'real time', and the devastation it would have caused my friend was enough to have shaken his time-space fabric, to the degree that it prompted a little reverberation, perhaps an echo, of this future blast. And this echo showed up visually, aurally, and viscerally in my friend's dream, on his mental screen."

"But what about the blast itself?" asked Dave.

"Ah, the blast itself," answered the Doctor, "was not in 'real time'. The blast itself originated in time <u>before</u> the dream...or perhaps concurrently <u>with</u> the dream but <u>before</u> the blast that singed my friend's fingers. Now there <u>is</u> the possibility that the bathroom blast <u>did</u> come first, and the dream was an echo and an afterimage of <u>that.</u> But you see what that does to your concept of time and events traveling on a <u>straightline</u> grid, in an <u>orderly</u> fashion from one point to the next? In the Time that I want you to comprehend there is no such order to events."

Dr. Berg picked up a cheap pocket watch which had been lying on the library table. He held it high and then brought it crashing down, crystal first on the table's surface. From beneath the smashed face he pulled a coiled mainspring and held it up, tossing the rest of the timepiece aside. He waved his hand above the spring, then beneath it.

"The event you just witnessed did not happen only here, or here." Dr. Berg then grasped the spring between his fingers and pointed to the outermost piece of the steel strip. "It happened here, at two o'clock," he pointed to the next inner band, "here at three o'clock," the next, "here at four o'clock," the next, "and it happened here at five o'clock, and all the way down the line. The watch no longer works <u>at any time</u>!" Dr. Berg took hold of the center piece and the outside end of the spring and pulled. His strong little fingers held one, long outstretched strip of steel.

"The event that ruined two o'clock, and destroyed three o'clock and stopped four o'clock, happened here! All at once!" He stood before the small group holding the outstretched spring for the point to hit home. His drama was received by complete silence from the awed group.

"Put aside past-present-future sequences," Dr. Berg continued in a more entreating manner. "Events just happen. And they can impinge upon one another, not necessarily by happening in any given <u>sequence</u>. Events can effect other events in <u>any</u> sequence. Pinpointing an occurrence to present, past or future is simply a convenience that appears to work for most men's purposes, but not necessarily for ours." Dr. Berg took a well deserved breath of the smoky air that had just begun to dissipate when he lit his Bjarne again.

"So the answer to Dave's question is yes, an event can reform and impinge upon us. The vibrations or shock of a blast that took place somewhere, someplace the OmniPlane reformed and were experienced in my friend's dream. Later all points coordinated on <u>our</u> spacetime grid and the event was seen and heard, and felt, to happen in my friend's hand. This was the event that crashed through the timespace barrier, because of its momentum and significance to my friend, and became manifest for <u>his</u> perceptions in <u>his</u> otherwise peaceful sleep. Possibly, Dave, it could also be captured on a piece of electromagnetic tape, or film or some other sensitive recording device, but the problem with that can be likened to the difficulty in capturing a whisper at one hundred yards using a sensitive microphone. The more sensitive it is the more it will pick up <u>everything</u> all along the hundred yards. The whisper itself gets obscured in the jumble. But events <u>can</u> reform themselves and <u>can</u> recur, either <u>after</u> or <u>before</u> they have occurred in the first place! They need not get lost in the jumble. And neither need the Time Traveler! Now, before we repair for some refreshment I should like to provide you notetakers and mapmakers with a broad outline of traveling options...for now. The details will follow."

Solly thought of what Timothy had been talking about before he disappeared. About certain powers not wanting any changes at this point in time, and about the two men who had appeared and then disappeared. And about Timothy. What the hell was all this business about 'Traveling' anyway? And where was Timothy?

"The options to which I cautiously refer," said the doctor, "can include: passing <u>through</u> an event on one level or time frame or space frame into another time frame or space frame, either instantly, or slowly; <u>vanishing</u> from one time or space event altogether into what is known as a UZ, an Uncharted Zone. This zone is uncharted with regard to space, time or existence as we know it; that is, with regard to its ever having existed. Another option can include: ceasing to be or <u>ever to have been</u>; or <u>coming into being</u> with no connection **to** any level or zone. I remind you" Berg looked out rather sternly into the group, "the consequence to any of these irregularities can be significant," he focused once again on his chair, rose and took a few short steps, "or can go virtually unnoticed." There was for some reason a common uneasiness in the room. Dr. Berg couldn't have helped but notice it. "There is only one place where a complete and reasonably accurate reproduction of an event that has taken place exists. Only one place where all the factors and ingredients remain correctly interrelated and undisturbed. Gentlemen, first I give you a phenomenon you will please permit me to call the OmniPlane. But it is the relationship between the OmniPlane and one other phenomenon that can allow us to travel...I should not say through, or even into, but more correctly onto time. Our friend Timothy established such a link. This other phenomenon to which I refer is that conduit of all we know, all there ever was to know and all we will ever know: **the mind.**" Dr. Berg stood up, took a gray tweed cap from the lace draped table and said, "And now gentlemen, let us repair to the Rackets."

THE RACKETS

Dr. Berg led the small group around a bend in his hallway and into an old and rather rickety elevator. It still had the round, little glass window on the door, with the chicken wire in the glass. Somehow Solly had not noticed the elevator earlier in the evening when he had made his ascent to apartment 4J. He had used the stairs. When the elevator reached the ground floor the light above the locally engraved door lit **M**, obviously for Mobius, thought Solly, and all were let out onto one of the two hallways which apparently led to the main lobby and front of the building. And so they all crossed the Persian tapestry, stepped outside and followed Dr. Berg around the corner into the Rackets, a relatively lively looking establishment, but one whose outside neon window sign read simply: **TAVERN**.

The bar in the Rackets extended from the entrance to the restroom at the back so if you had a few beers while working your way along the barstools, by the time you got through saying 'hello' you'd be right where you wanted to be. But Solly didn't know too many people at the bar that night so he remained about where he started, two or three stools from the front door. Dave's was the only other familiar face nearby. The rest of Dr. Berg's little group, including Dr. Berg, had melted into the crowd. Solly paid for his brew and ambled toward Dave.

"So where the hell is Mortimers?"   Solly said to Dave.

"If you turn the corner from the front of Berg's building, you should wind up at Mortimers. But I didn't see it at all."

"Mortimers? Where the hell is <u>Mortimers</u>?" said Dave. "Where the hell is the <u>Rackets</u>?"

"I don't quite follow," said Solly after a considerable pause. Dave took a swig from his bottle.

"You think any of us really understand what's going on here? I don't quite know what the game is but so far as I'm concerned it's take the credit and run."

"Credit?"

"Dr. Berg promised some of us extra credit if we sat in on his night lectures and went along on these little experiments of his, but frankly, it's all still pretty much of a mystery...to everybody." Another pause. "I mean the lectures are interesting and all, but I'm in the dark. And I haven't the slightest idea how he does it. How he gets to this place like he does."

"What do you mean?"

"I mean you can't find this place during the day, or for that matter at night, without Berg. It doesn't seem to exist! We've all tried already. You can't find the damn place. But when we file out of the building with Berg, we just make that right turn around the corner, like we did tonight, just as neat and simple as you please, and shit! There it is. The Tavern. Everybody in here calls it the Rackets. And Mortimers is nowhere in sight....And <u>nobody in here ever seems to have heard of Mortimers</u>!"

"Jesus!"

"Right." So we keep on coming. At least it's interesting. There must be a logical explanation. I don't know how <u>simple</u> it'll be, but it's got to be logical. Especially for Dr. Berg." Dave seemed to ponder this last thought rather soberly. He drained the remainder of his beer and shook his head ever so slightly several times. "He's such a...logical man."

Dave's trailing away could not have come at a more perfect moment. Solly had just seen something at the end of the bar that startled him. The bartender...the face on the bartender belonged to Timothy. Solly felt a wave of dizziness. It wasn't the beer either. There had been two or three men tending bar when Solly and his company had come in. Solly had only observed one of them carefully and he was certain neither of the others looked familiar in the least. Surely he would have recognized Tim. Quickly Solly stepped toward the far end of the bar...although he tried not to be obvious. Sure enough Timothy, apron clad and wiping a glass, put his head down.

"Sshh," he cautioned. "Not too much fuss."

"What in the world are you doing here? What are you doing tending bar? I can't believe this," Solly said plaintively, knowing full well what an understatement it was. "Is somebody going to tell me what the hell is going on?"

"What kind of brew was that sir?" asked Timothy.

"Draught. Give me your best draught."

"Draught it is sir. Bass. How about a Bass?"

"Bass. Good," said Solly. "Bass. Make it a Bass."

It did not take someone of Timothy's nimble witt to perceive that Solly was annoyed and rapidly becoming unnerved.

"Well, I'll tell you this much," said Timothy leaning forward as he put a foaming half pint of Bass Ale on the bar in front of Solly, "I don't work here on weekends."

"What does that mean?"

"It means," continued Timothy in a low voice, "I'm not moonlighting. I guess you got to meet Dr. Berg."

"Well, if you can call sitting in on one of his lectures for fortyfive minutes meeting him. I thought we were going to talk about you."

"You were. After the lecture. Down here. But I can see that's not going to happen. Not tonight anyway."

"Why not?"

"Look carefully at the man in the tweed cap. He's drinking what you're drinking."

"I **know.** That's Berg. So?"

"I said look carefully. That's not Dr. Berg. It's not the man you walked in here with either."

It was at that very moment the stocky man in the tweed cap turned toward the bar and Solly. It wasn't Dr. Berg. Solly felt more than uneasiness in the pit of his stomach. "So? So it's not Berg. Maybe he went to the restroom for a moment. What is this place anyway?"

"This place," said Timothy as he wiped a small area of bar surface, "is a kind of safe house. It's part of Berg's training program really. At least it started out that way. Now it's <u>supposed</u> to be a safe house. But you couldn't have got here by yourself."

"Some safe house." Solly was looking around the smoky room for Berg but there was no sign of him.

"I wouldn't be too concerned at the moment, Solly. Dr. Berg knows his way around better than anyone. He's quite capable of taking care of himself and taking, let's say, evasive action. I promise you'll see him again. But for now just slip off your stool and kind of mingle your way to the door. Wait for me under the amber light in the alcove. A little while ago you asked me why I was here. Well, for the past several days I've been trying to avoid someone. Apparently I'm not doing a very good job of it. I don't understand how they're doing it but they seem to know every move I make. Now, I think it's time to make another move, with <u>you.</u> Keep an eye on the man in the tweed cap and try not to let him get too close to you. Wait at the amber light until you hear the phone ring. It won't ring very loudly. Step inside the booth and pick up the phone."

Timothy stepped backward, turned, and disappeared behind a panel of mirrors. Solly made his way toward the dimly lit alcove and its wooden phonebooth. Nothing but a small, blank bulletin board was apparent in the stark little nook, a dull amber light overhead and the dark brown booth. In fact, Solly was struck by how visually spare the space was. There was no sign, no ads, no phone books, no vending machines. Nothing. Just the booth. The phone rang. Solly picked up the receiver and unfolded the wood and glass door shut. The little fan wedged in the upper left hand corner started whirring as Solly heard Timothy's voice.

"Listen carefully. There's a nasty game of tag going on here. A couple of guys known as 'farmers' are looking for me and, I suspect, you, particularly before I get to fill you in on a few matters of some urgency. So far I've managed to lose one of them, but the other one is in this room sipping an ale. He's the one looking like Berg. Now I don't know where Berg is but I know he can fend for himself. As soon as I come out to you we're going to make a hasty exit. I'm talking to you on the phone right now because there are a few instructions I have to tell you before we leave and I would rather not arouse any suspicion or undue attention. Can you hear me all right?"

"Yes. Fine. Why are these guys called 'farmers'?"

"Because they're here to plant seeds and remove weeds. You understand? And I'm a weed. I think they see <u>you</u> as a weed too."

"But why? What have I done?"

"I can't go into it now, but you're involved. For the moment just hear me out." Solly's senses bristled. His ear was pressed to the receiver. He was paying very close attention. He was also shivering a little. "The difference between everyday living and time travel..."

"Time travel?"

"Please, Solly. The difference is that in everyday living, envisioning things and believing in them can and does make them happen, at least eventually, depending on the strength of your vision, mental energy and will. In time travel you also envision. But it all has to happen **now!** Everything is vision and energy but it must happen **now.** But you can't try too hard, Solly. Try and understand this. It's a real casual, laid back, process. You just do it. If you think about it for a moment you lose it. Nothing will click. That's really what most of Berg's training is about. Believing. It's a matter of believing **where** you're going **and going directly there.** There can't be a hair's breadth of a doubt. That will throw you off course. It's an exercise in positive concentration. Learning how to **travel** is like learning how to ride a two wheeler for the first time. You've got to **believe** in it. One look back, one doubt, and you fall. It's like believing in diseases or cures. You can either get them or get rid of them. Berg actually believes he can get **to** anywhere **from** anywhere. Hang up now Solly....I'm coming to get you. Stay in the booth."

Within moments Timothy came through the alcove portal. "Let's try for the fifties, Solly. Remember? I'm going to follow you so the choice is up to you. Do you feel strong about the late fifties? A special night in the village with your college chums? Looking for a couple of lovelies? Can you remember, Solly? We don't have too much time."

"Give me a moment to think," said Solly. His mind was almost there as he uttered the words.

"Don't think too much. Just get the picture and let's go. Remember, no negative vibes. Not one. It'll be like trying not to think of a red elephant...but just try." Timothy glanced at his watch, then through the closed alcove portal. The man in the tweed cap that resembled Berg's was still nursing his pint of ale and had begun looking around the room, through the smoke. "Ready? Let's go."

Solly took hold of the cast iron handle and latch and pushed the front door to the Rackets open. He then stepped somewhat cautiously into the street. But as he did so he couldn't help embracing the image of himself, along with Dr. Berg and the others earlier in the evening traversing these very steps, only in reverse. Timothy was close behind.

"Whoops," said Timothy, somewhat uncharacteristically. I don't think you made it." Solly looked around. It was pretty much the same street he remembered coming down earlier. It was the street leading to Berg's place around the corner. But it was very still and very quiet. There were no passersby in sight.

"Maybe you could tell me what's going on?"

"If I told you absolutely nothing that would be close," Timothy chuckled. "But the fact that we did not get into your 1950's might make it a bit easier for them to find us. All, however, is not lost. We can try again later. This time you'll follow me. You know the 42nd Street Library?" Timothy chuckled again. He was apparently enjoying himself.

"Of course."

"The South reading room?"

"Yes...."

"Good. Let's go there. There's something I should like to show you."

Somehow, without noticing just how it happened, they got to 40th Street much quicker than Solly had anticipated. Perhaps it was Timothy's conversation. He had insisted on making a few points, and perhaps the talk had eaten up the time. Meanwhile, all along the way, the night street was immersed in an eerie stillness.

"Why the hell is it so quiet," Solly asked?

"Didn't you ever notice while walking down any street, smack in the middle of a busy day, suddenly everything seems to come to a halt for a moment? It's especially noticeable to the ears. For a few split seconds there is no noise, no traffic movement, no horns, no yelling. Almost nothing. Then, just as you become aware of the silence, it breaks.

Horns, voices, thuds. Everything is back. And you wonder how it all could come to have been silent for those few moments. You wonder if it was your imagination. Well, it was not. The moments of quiet are brought about when someone or something is **traveling.** Depending on the scope of who or what is passing through, a rearrangement takes place in time and in space. A realigning, you might say. Oh, sometimes it's very slight. Infinitesimal. You would hardly notice, It's like making an insert or deletion into a page or paragraph on your wordprocessor. As the change is made there is a realignment. It's quick and it's silent. But just <u>before</u> the change takes place there is a moment, an instant, where everything is frozen. It is at that very fraction of time that one can, if one is astute, become aware of the telltale silence indicative of the **prealignment moment.** And tonight, Solly, you may not know it yet, but we are in the midst of traveling. Right now, thanks to Dr. Berg, we're walking through a rather large launch window. There are still a few things however, I want you to work on." Solly thought perhaps he might be working on too much already. "You have got to <u>believe,</u> Solly. When a 747 takes off into the blue sky, how many people aboard that aircraft do you think <u>don't</u> believe it's going to get off the ground? And who's to say what the result would be if that <u>were</u> the case? There are those, in fact, Solly, who believe if it weren't for <u>their</u> collective energies and will, that 747 would not take off at all!" Timothy began fumbling for his pipe. "Did you know a small nucleus of physicians hold to the theory that if men actually believed and I say 'men' because man's belief is predicated on what men, collectively, believe if men believed that a severed leg could be regrown it could be done! But we don't <u>believe</u> it, so it can't be done! Some of nature's lower species don't know any better, so they do it. They go right ahead and re-grow appendages." Timothy stopped dead in his tracks. Solly looked up, following Timothy's stare and stood transfixed, at what he saw.

As the two of them had approached 40th Street, lifting their eyes, Solly had expected them to see the library, hovering in the night above street level, its promenade steps flanked by the two familiar stone lions placidly overlooking Fifth Avenue. Instead there was no library. But there, inbetween 40th Street and 42nd Street, overwhelming against the empty darkness backed by boundless sky, was the awesome Croton Reservoir, its fortyfour foot walls of granite gaping at the night. Clumps of greenery, hedges of sorts, crouched before the Eastern wall while clinging ivy stretched to climb parts of her Northern wall. It was difficult to comprehend whether it was the impressive Croton Reservoir, like the base of a giant pyramid, or the terribly painful absence of the 42nd Street Library that was more astonishing.

THE LIBRARY

The moment had come unexpectedly for Solly. He thought he was in a trance. Up the block, across the street from the reservoir was what appeared to be a large and beautifully ornate apartment building, at least seven stories high. It could even have been a hotel or lodging house. It was difficult to tell in the darkness. Most of the windows had little awnings. Almost all of the shades and curtains or draperies were drawn. Across the way, to the east, high above almost everything, were the twin towers of what must have been the old Temple Emanu-El. And, far in the distance, Solly could just barely make out the spires of Saint Patrick's Cathedral.

"Solly! Pull yourself together for a moment. Try to recall the library. I'm glad you stumbled into this, but you've got to keep moving. Follow me around to where the library's 42nd Street side entrance used to...ah...is going to be." The pair made haste despite Solly's twirling about in attempts to take it all in. They walked to the far side of the clinging ivy. It was approximately dead center of the reservoir's northern wall. Built into the wall was an entrance of sorts. Leading up to the entrance were a half dozen steps. Timothy faced Solly. "Now, Solly, tell me about the library. Turn around, look at the Hotel Bristol, and tell me about the library. How often did you study here?" Solly turned to face the Bristol, tried to count the stories, and found himself looking into the sky.

"Well, I used to come primarily on weekends. We'd show up at about ten in the morning and stay until ten at night. There used to be a Bickfords Restaurant on Fifth Avenue. Sometimes we'd eat there. Other times we'd eat at this new fastfood steakhouse called Tads farther west on 42nd. Sometimes dinner would be at one of the nearby Automats. I remember the reading rooms. The little cards you got with the numbers on them. Waiting for your number to light up on the board in front so you could come up to claim your book. I remember the long wooden tables, the green shaded lights, the hard oak chairs, the sound they made against the floor when you got up. I remember the faces across the table in front of you, and those to the side, across the aisle. I remember the little book carts, the card catalogues, the slips, the piles and stacks of books and the 3 by 5s. All the little rubberbanded collections of 3 by 5s. And I remember the notebooks. The doodled in and doodled upon notebooks."

Timothy had inserted something into the lock on the door before him. "Solly," he said, "we're going to back in. Trust me. And keep talking. I like your story."

Solly started telling about the time he and a friend thought it might be a good idea to ride the lions. But before he could get too deeply into it Timothy was tugging him back, or forward as the case may be. For when he turned around he was peering across the security check out counters positioned at the side entrance of the New York 42nd Street Library. "How the hell did you do that? And what about the alarm?"

"This was before alarms, remember?" Timothy smiled his mischievous smile.

"But...the Reservoir? How did we get into the Library?"

"Because the only thing you and I have ever known to exist behind that door is right here. Where we're standing right now. The only thing you could ever <u>really</u> imagine to be behind that door is...this. We made it happen, Solly. You and I."

"What about the Reservoir appearing out of nowhere...and the street...and all those old buildings?"

"They were, or <u>are</u> all part of one scene in time. Let's start up to the main reading room and I'll try to explain." The two of them stepped out into the corridor and began the two story climb up the polished stone stairs and on to the third floor. They turned right, walked down the long marble hall, flanked by delicate wood and glass display cases, and on to room 315, the card catalogue room, at the end of which would be the two main reading rooms...South and North. Moonlight found its way into the large hallways and main reading rooms through the segmental arch windows creating strange patterns of shadows. The contrasts between the lights and darks were startling. But for the moonlight and the shadows it would have been perfectly black inside. Solly thought to himself if it <u>had</u> been <u>perfectly</u> black none of the myriad ideas would exist for anyone scanning the shelves. Or <u>could</u> ideas exist without illumination? Solly enjoyed toying with the word. Perhaps ideas themselves were illumination enough. He followed Timothy into one of the two main reading rooms where they sat down.

'*And stood awhile in uffish thought*,' Solly mumbled to himself.

"Beg pardon?" responded Timothy as if awakened out of a slight reverie himself.

"Nothing. A line from a Lewis Carroll poem. Lines from it seem to keep cropping up inside my head. I get the feeling it bears some connection with something or other. I just don't know quite what yet."

"Well...,"said Timothy, breathing out a long sigh, "here we sit." Above him sprawled that magnificient dome of ornate creation. Somehow it all seemed appropriate. "This seems to be <u>the</u> place for truth and beauty in the world. That's why I took you here Solly. Ever notice those two statues on either side of the main entrance? The man on the Sphinx is truth; the woman on Pegasus is beauty. Truth and Beauty. It's all here. And this is the one place our foes, those exponents of everything that stands against truth, everything that defies and besmirches beauty, could not tolerate. They could not survive in here. There is too much truth within these walls, too many ideas, too much good. Now, let me tell you how we got here. Hold on to your seat."

"Albert Einstein said space had shape and could therefore be bent or curved. Well, similarly, Time has shape and can be indelibly impressed on any one of its several facets, levels or layers, by events which can create such an impact through sheer force or beauty. Devastation can do it; magnificient architecture can do it; tragic grief can do it; overwhelming joy can do it." For the moment Solly had lost all sense of time. **And for damn good reason**, he thought. "Moments," Timothy continued, "instances or even entire decades are shaped by these forces. And Time itself is impressed forever. **If something of considerable substance occurs just once, it can live forever in Time.** And the more powerful, the more beautiful or overwhelming its force, and its character, the deeper its imprint and the more prominent its physical place in Time. Also the more easily it can be retrieved, and the more readily it stands to remanifest itself in one form or another."

Images of people and events began a slow jog through Solly's mind. He thought of warriors who had sworn they fought the same or similar battles on the same battlefields in another life. He thought of catastrophic events that had ravaged the same little towns more than once. He thought of significant events happening years apart, yet bearing great coincidental factors in common, like the Lincoln and Kennedy assassinations. Both presidents shot in the head from behind. Both shot on a Friday. Both killed by assassins born nearly one hundred years apart. Both succeeded by men, Southern Democrats named Johnson, born almost exactly one hundred years apart. Lincoln elected to the congress in 1846, Kennedy in 1946. Lincoln becoming President in 1860, Kennedy in 1960. Then there was Kennedy's secretary, Lincoln, and Lincoln's secretary Kennedy, both warning the chief executives not to pursue their schedules, which turned out to be those fatal appointments with destiny. Neither assassin stood trial. Both were shot. Solly had anticipated Timothy's next directive which startled him from his reverie.

" Think about it Solly. Great events have done it. Great battles. Great people. Heroic or heinous deeds. Great decades have done it. The shape and scope, the capacity and variation of Time is limitless. She is no unbroken NorthSouth line but an eternally multiphased mosaic.

Look around you Solly. Try to get the overwhelming sense of it. All creation passes through her, changing her shape, Some pieces in the mosaic are altered more effectively than other pieces. Some become indelible. **And when Time embraces something wondrous or beautiful, or something catastrophic, she will never, for all eternity, let it go.** That something will recur again and again, and it will be unmistakable. Its identity shall never be lost nor forgotten. The sands may shift but shall always come back to be drawn round these great events and forces in the mantle of Time. Just like the sun bends nearby light and space, and causes passing objects to be drawn toward it, across its sloping space, so these great events and monuments shape and bend Time to guide and influence all that cross her many embracing and inescapable horizons." If there wasn't a distinct chill in the reading room, you could have fooled Solly. Then, out of nowhere, as if it were an afterthought from another conversation Timothy said, "Ghosts? You bet I believe in ghosts!" He added, "what I am talking about has been given many names through the years: ghosts, coincidence, apparition, superstition, magic, miracles, luck. But there are more amazing,terrifying and wondrous things than that! It is what is true...if you can accept it for what it is...truth. And not by any other name."

The two of them sat there in the immense South reading room under its magnificient dome high overhead. The library was, Solly thought somewhat sarcastically, almost as quiet as he had remembered it during reading hours on those hushed weekend afternoons. But actually, the South reading room on this night was probably the stillest surrounding in which he had ever been enveloped. It was quieter than Llareggub Hill in the wee hours. Timothy kipled back in his chair, came forward again and clasped his hands on the table, leaning in toward Solly.

"Now I'm going to tell you why we are here and what we are going to do. We're at a crossroads of sorts. There's a fork on the grid. Berg and I have worked it out, although you don't need to be a precise mathematician to know what's going on today, and where it's leading or where it originated. But that's my terrain: where it came from. Your job will be more at stopping what we're already stuck with, and preventing it from going any further. But the tricky part, Solly, is that we're at a critical stage here. There's simply no more time left. Things have gone too far already. Basically we're trying to stop two people, and their creations. One of them has gotten quite out of hand, which complicates things. And one event will always lead to another. So I've got to try to go back even farther than we had planned and interfere at an earlier stage. What do the letters SS convey to you?"

"Secret Service?"

"Good. What else?"

"Nazi Storm Trooper?"

"Right. The correct word is Schutzsstaffel. It was first instituted as a kind of Defense Corps or Security Staff. Of course, it turned into quite something else. How about another SS?

"I don't know....Social Security?"

"Right again. And you know something? They're all related. The letters SS insist upon finding their mark again and again. Like they're trying to tell us something. And nobody seems to be listening."

'It will recur again and again, Solly thought, It will be unmistakable. The sands may shift but shall always come home.'

"But," said Solly, "couldn't that really, simply, be coincidence?"

"Coincidence? There is an active law in the universe which tends toward **unity.** Do you recall a great Austrian genius named Paul Kammerer? He devoted a good part of his life to the study of what we call coincidence. He discovered that this universal force acts selectively on form and function to <u>bring similar configurations together in space and time.</u> In our universe things are correlated by affinity. Coincidences are not accidental. Kammerer identified them as 'cyclic processes which propagate themselves like waves along the timeaxis of the spacetime continuum'. And with a little traveling I dare say you will find that he was right."

"And what about 'SS'?"

"SS is coming around to take its place, rightful or not, to make another one of its recurring marks...a deep one this time, on the mantle. That's what we hope to stop."

"I'm not quite sure I follow," said Solly. "Social Security is...well, a salvation to millions of people."

"Yes," said Timothy slowly, "salvation. You might call it that. But at whose hands? Consider whom you had to shake hands with to get that ...salvation? And look at the price it has already cost, in terms of your freedom, your identity, your privacy, not to mention what it will be about to cost us all....Very soon! Salvation? How about Satanic Salvation?"

Solly swallowed uneasily.

"You see, the Schutzstaffel was also initially instituted to protect and defend. A Defense or Security Corps. Initially,...another of its purposes was to provide work for the unemployed. That's one reason it attracted so many Brown Shirts. By 1932 about 300,000 of its members came from the ranks of the unemployed. And by then it had already turned into a private Nazi Army. They're not exactly Nazis ...yet, but the Office of the Secret Service hasn't exactly spawned an internationally beloved clique of sweethearts." Solly glanced at his watch. Almost two a.m. But it had been almost two a.m. for some time now. "Plenty of time," said Timothy. "Don't worry about the time in here.

The initial intentions behind Social Security," he continued, "were admirable. But the number...that <u>number,</u> has been taken too far. When choice is replaced by mandate, when there are no options, only requirements, watch out. We are being filed, <u>every one of us</u>, and we will eventually be restricted, altered and neatly put away, in that order. Codified, modified and podified!

Not too long ago there was an arch conservative woman legislator who, for whatever reasons of her own, and they usually are personal, was obsessed with introducing legislation taking our little number a step or two further. The idea, under the guise of protecting U.S. citizens from incoming hordes of illegal aliens, was to have all legitimate, bonafide citizens carry with them, at all times, an identification card. Failure to produce the card would most certainly have resulted in trouble. The legislation did get passed and we were all required to carry the card. At first it was simply used as convenient identification. But it was not long before its abuses became legion. Virtually nothing could be obtained or ascertained without the card. No distance could be traversed, no action could transpire, without the card. But, I daresay, you cannot recall this, can you? You yourself had such a card prominently displayed under a safe celluloid window in your Florentine wallet." Timothy leaned back into a kiple again, grinning. "But, you don't anymore.... Do you?"

"I never had such a card!"

"And I'll tell you something else you don't have any longer. You don't know what I'm talking about...because you no longer have any memory of the card...the Citizen I.D. Card...! Do you?" Solly, somewhat perplexed, decided to look in his wallet for some inexplicable reason. He flipped it open and looked at the clear window. There was nothing behind it. Other than that, however, his wallet was jammed. He found it strange he should have had nothing displayed in that prime slot under the window. He showed the open billfold before Timothy. Timothy nodded."I know," he said. "You see, we can make a few modifications of our own. Of course some our friends back there are on to me, and Berg, and you too. It seems they've been around the block a few times themselves. But once we accomplish what we must, there won't be too much they can do about it. We will set them back years...and we will introduce a terrible confusion into their system. This time everything is in our favor. It's much easier to undo than to do. Entropy is on our side this time. We're the ones introducing the virus."

"You said you've got to go back again to stop something from getting out of hand?"

"Well, it's already out of hand. I'm going back to see what I can do about the **number.** It won't be an easy trip though. There are too many powerful and brutal people waiting to stop me. They're guarding that number very carefully. They've been watching and waiting for this a very long time. But I think I'm ready. Just keep watching your wallet."

"And what about <u>me</u>? Am I ready?"

"What you're after isn't off the drawing board yet. And I don't think they're anticipating a move in that direction. Not just now anyway. Ever hear of EFT? Of course you have. Electronic Funds Transfer. Well, if these people have their way, especially one of them, whom you're going to meet, a Mr. Raymond Gomez of Chemical American Bank, pretty soon we'll be carrying a PTC... Personal Transfer Card."

'Beware the Jabberwock, my son, the jaws that bite, the claws that catch...' The phrase sounded in Solly's head quite independently.

"You just dip the card into one of those nice machines" Timothy continued, "and your **State** account will be debited or credited according to the transaction you've just accomplished. If you worked...you'll be credited. If you just received a service or made a purchase, your account will be debited. Soon tax filing will become obsolete because they'll know everything you've <u>bought,</u> all you've <u>earned,</u> everywhere you've <u>been</u> and everything you've <u>done.</u> They will know **every transaction** you made...and...with **whom!** They will know your whereabouts at every moment. They will be able to reconstruct your every activity. **They will be able to reconstruct your life!** Power will be very limited because money and spending is power. And those two items will be very carefully watched and controlled. In fact, Solly, eventually it won't matter <u>what</u> you earn because you'll never see any of the money anyway. If you need anything that costs beyond what you have earned, you simply go into a debit balance, within certain limits, for it. Savings plans will, naturally, after at first having been carefully monitored and guided, regulated and stabilized, with minimums and maximums, limits and ceilings, be phased out. Because, basically, there will have been an erosion of both need...and incentive."

"Sounds like an evolution into the pure communist ideal: Each works according to his ability and draws from the system or state according to his needs."

"But it's worse than that, Solly. Where is the incentive to work according to one's ability? There won't be any. And the system will fail. <u>Everything</u> will fail! But before total collapse, the state will try to implement some drastic amendments to the system. Two major changes will occur. first, the Personal Funds Transfer Card becomes the Collective Funds Transfer Card. It's one big bank account and it belongs to everybody. Naturally it's quite regulated and restricted by the state and every transaction will be a nightmare of financial paperwork or their equivalent to paperwork. There will be lines, interminable waiting, red tape and bureaucratic entanglements unlike anything remotely tolerable. Of course it won't be because the system will be incapable of handling what they have wrought. Never think that! The hidden purpose of the massive, frustrating delays is to discourage and dissuade <u>casual</u> use of funds and the wasting of precious state time, which brings me to the second major change. This will also involve a card...a direct descendant of the FTC item Mr. Gomez is soon to be working on."

Solly looked at his watch again. It was still almost two a.m.

"I told you we have plenty of time," Timothy grinned. "But we shall be leaving quite shortly. Don't you want to know about the card you're going to stop from ever existing...at least for the, shall we say, <u>forseeable</u> future?"

"I'm not altogether sure, Timothy. Do you really think I'm ready to do anything about all of this?"

"You're more ready than you know or, pardon the expression, credit yourself for. Let me tell you about this most nightmarish innovation. It will be known as your Liesure Card. With it you will be checked in and out of every activity, work or play, and will be allowed just so much unproductive time. Any time <u>not strictly accounted for</u>, that is, <u>utilized without state approval</u> will be heavily taxed. <u>Sanctioned</u> liesure time will merely be taxed at standard rates. Utilizing your Liesure Pass will enable you to come and go, freely, from your residence, not just your state, city and neighborhood boundaries. Yes, productivity <u>will</u> be enforced, to remain high. Time will not be wasted. Waste <u>will</u> be taxed and penalized. Or so they think."

"How could such a nightmare happen?"

"It's already begun. Don't you have to show passes to gain entry to office buildings in large cities? Don't you find yourself signing in and out of places? Had your picture taken lately? Been on TV at the bank, department store credit window, supermarket, or your local elevator, coming and going? Some of those records exist on tape, you know. Ah...but just for the record, of course! You'll soon find yourself signing in at parks, museums, theaters, public malls, shopping plazas, even your own apartment building! In fact, some buildings already make it a practice to sign tenants in and out, together with the times of their entries and departures. The doormen do it, quietly of course. The procedures are already in practice. It's all there, just waiting to be formalized...and then enforced. First they'll sell it as a convenient <u>once-and-for-all</u> identity card. Sort of a domestic passport, you know,good for all kinds of situations. It might not even be mandatory at first. Then those who don't have one will find themselves pressured, locked out of places that call for the card to gain entry. No tickee, no washee. You'll be asked to show two forms of identification. One of them will be the card. It might even be required to get a job. You won't really <u>have</u> to have one. But, no card, no job! Sound familiar? Just another shifting of the sands. At first not many people will object. In fact, some will see it as a kind of priviledge. Others will eventually give in. But, initially, few will object. Later it will be too late. Checkpoints will be everywhere. Gates will be opened only by **The Card.** People will at last flock, on their own, to obtain the thing...because, finally, the greatest fear will be that of having your Liesure Card confiscated, revoked, not renewed, unless you, Solly, unless you find Mr Gomez...and lose Mr. Gomez." Timothy pushed his chair back, making a loud reverberating noise throughout the entire South reading room, and rose. "Let us leave now and set our clocks straight."

THE LIONS

The long third floor corridor was both lovely and eerie in the faint night light that filtered through to that dignified hallway. But most notable perhaps was the brittle stillness that pervaded the hall's essence from one end to the other. This time, however, the pair of night invaders did not walk to the hall's far end, by which way they had come. Timothy had said he felt it would be better if they had exited the hallowed premises through the front, before the waiting lions. So the two men began a slow descent of the main, central marble staircase. Neither Solly nor Timothy were aware of how prescient Timothy's remark regarding the waiting lions was.

"Two questions," said Solly.

"Okay."

"How the hell did you pull that vanishing stunt in the park the other day?"

"Simple. Berg and I for a long time had had the location marked and charted. The table you and I were sitting at is on the exact spot where a couple of giant boulders years ago formed a kind of alcove. The whole area was obscured by a thicket. It all went when the boat basin and the cake house were built. But I knew the spot was there, and when I glimpsed the two farmers closing in I used the alcove for cover. They didn't know about the spot and couldn't see me. Neither could anyone else...in this decade. The technique was similar to the one we used tonight. But, I dare say, had you known about the boulders you <u>could</u> have seen me very well. It would have been no trick to you at all! You might say...the boulder is all in the eye of the beholder." Solly groaned. Timothy had some playful, and sometimes rather painful, linguistic habits, especially to the <u>ear</u> of the beholder. "Second question?"

"Tell me candidly," asked Solly, "how do you come by your knowledge of tomorrow?"

"Dr. Berg mostly," answered Timothy. "He has a device. A scanner. What he likes to call his link. Its operation utilizes sensors to <u>detect</u> light, electricity, movement, impulses of all kinds, sound, radio waves. Just about everything that our immediate environment comprises. That which emanates from our world. That which constitutes our world...today. <u>All</u> of it. But the scanner has to filter all of these stimuli <u>from</u> our current state of affairs. It has to eliminate, neutralize, disregard and discriminate until <u>today</u> is filtered out. No amplitude modulation, frequency modulation, short waves, long waves, xrays, gamma, ultra violet. Nothing! Only then can the scanner receive what Berg describes as some rather fine, delicate and rare transmissions. Finally, after the primary system of sensors and filters clears a path for these transmissions, the scanner's secondary unit of tuning and enhancement comes into play. With <u>that</u> Berg is able to reproduce, if we can use the word 'reproduce', tomorrow."

They had come to the bottom of the landing on the second floor. Timothy looked down both sides of the quiet corridor. It was so still. Then from the outside a light pierced the panes of glass in the hall below. It was <u>not</u> from the brilliant moon. And it had not been there before. Timothy and Solly began to descend toward the main lobby, a bit more slowly, but neither mentioned the light outside. Timothy continued with what he had been saying.

"It all started in one of those sensory deprivation chambers. You know, no light, no sound, no movement, no smells. Totally sterile. Berg had set up his instruments there. He had been working with some particularly sensitive ones. They were capable not only of <u>detecting</u> the faintest and most minute stimuli, but in gathering and recording them in batches. He mixed and matched countless combinations of lenses and filters, and repeatedly amplified and refined the sound transmissions he received until something quite new and unique was detected. Eventually

Dr. Berg began sending like impulses back...or forward...along the same route from which his signals had come. The path we traced was circuitous, to say the least. Berg confirmed that our universe is indeed mathematically one of no less than eleven dimensions. Seven, in fact, are so infinitesimal as to have curled up upon themselves, each characteristic perhaps a direct result of the other; each feeding off the other, so to speak. It's difficult to say. Anyway the path of his recorded extratime was traced. And he was able to relay messages back along his traced path. Using high energy impulses Berg actually was able to catch up with and reach tiny tachyons, the particles of which time is made, in flight."

"Do you really subscribe to the notion that just because we know light can be broken down into photons, time can be broken down into particles too? Tachyons?"

"And space. And everything else. Time is no exception. But it's not one of the infinitesmal seven dimensions. We keep time up here with us. She's one of the top four dimensions. So she's still relatively accessible. Tachyons. Little, tiny, wavelike fellas. And Berg caught up with some of them."

"That must have been some bundle of equipment. I wouldn't like to be on the receiving end of one of his requisitions."

"Well the original package was cumbersome and bulky. And simulating the kind of environment in which he felt he needed to work wasn't easy. But microchips simplified matters. Now the whole business fits inside that transparent pen he carries. He doesn't need his sensory deprivation chamber anymore either. No need to sterilize the environment. The pen does it all. It works anywhere by completely cutting out today, and tuning in... tomorrow! It's like his private telephone to the future, or the past. He even has a little acronym for it: **TOC TIC.** Tune out chaos...tune in chronos. Seems he's reached the point where he can find out exactly what's going on anywhere, anytime. And then he gets there, not much differently than by our methods. For him though, it's a lot easier. You see, when you can hear the sounds and see the images, when you <u>know</u> it's all <u>there,</u> getting there is much less effort. In fact, Solly, virtually nothing is out of the way for Berg. You might say that although his reach is quite extensive, it does not exceed his grasp."

"Surely there's a catch somewhere. There always is."

"Most assuredly."

"And...?"

"One hates to think of it, much less dwell upon it. But the frustrating fact is Berg wasn't the only one to happen on his discoveries. It's not clear where, nor, of course, <u>when,</u> the like discoveries were made but we are not alone in the game. And somehow it has all come to the attention of the farmers. There's almost no place to which we can travel where, and when, we don't run into them. They're like a plague. Locusts. Army ants. And Berg especially has to maintain a very low profile. I'm afraid what little anonymity I had enjoyed for awhile is eroding. That's why we've recruited you, Solly. They don't quite know you...yet. It <u>will</u> change. But not before it will be too late for them."

They had reached the last of the stone steps. Timothy pushed open the front doors after unlocking them from the inside. The two men breathed in the damp early morning air and started down toward the street. There was a black car parked in front of the library. Two men got out on either side of the car and started briskly up the steps toward the library entrance. Timothy's and Solly's attentions were now riveted in the now somewhat ominous direction of the lions.

"Do you still have my leather notebook?"

"Yes."

"When you're alone, remove the front and back covers. They slide off. Inside are some fifty and one hundred dollar bills. See that Raymond Gomez of the Chemical American Bank gets the money. I believe the bank is now called...CHEMERA"

"How?" The men were closing in.

"Put them on his desk. Try to make a deposit. Just get him to see that money. Now...when I tell you, make a break. Run for the Park Avenue tunnel. See if you can find the door along the mini walk on the right heading south. It's about two thirds of the way into the tunnel. The rest is in the notebook. You'll understand it now."

Timothy was talking very rapidly. The two men were on his level now. The larger man on the right, grabbed Timothy's sleeve. He seemed to ignore Solly, as did his partner.

"Timothy Gillis?"

Timothy did not respond but instead continued talking to Solly. "Don't forget our friend. <u>Lose our friend!</u> Go Solly," he yelled. "Now! Go south!" And Solly took off, two steps at a leap...like a bat.

'Beware the Jubjub bird, and shun the frumious Bandersnatch.'

"Solly!" one of the men screamed as if to awaken the night. Sol Learner, stop!" This second man also flew down the steps and onto Fifth Avenue, galloping after Solly. "You won't get far!," he yelled. "You won't get far!"

Solly took a right just short of the corner and then climbed back onto the little pedestrian walkway before the grand edifice. He doubled back toward the lions. The man who had taken hold of Timothy must have had thoughts of intercepting the runner as he leapt backward between the two great stone beasts. The smaller man was close behind Solly.

At that instant Solly, who had begun to see a strange flickering around the library from the moment he had begun his run, saw more clearly just where he was headed. Before him, right behind the lions, was the shimmering, flickering entrance to the Croton Reservoir that he had so vividly seen before. He thought of what Timothy had related about the alcove beneath their table at the park cafe, ran towards what he saw now, and ducked in the shadows of the Reservoir doorway.

When the man who had been holding Timothy emerged from between the lions, Solly was nowhere in sight. The man's breathless partner rejoined him and the two of them bundled Timothy into their vehicle. Then they scanned the scene once again. There was not a sound and no indication at all of Solly. "Crap!", said the smaller man who took the wheel as the larger, man sat with Timothy in the back. The engine turned over and the car, burning some oil, sped off downtown and into the night. On the bottom of the license plate were the numbers 1946. It had just begun to rain and the streets had already begun to shine.

TUNNELS

Solly felt the dirty New York rain on his face, watched it wet down the street, heard the forty year old car take off and stepped out from what he had just thought was his cover. But it was no more. Contemporary Fifth Avenue lay before him, the library stood behind him and he was getting doused standing out in the open. The night, in fact, seemed to vanish behind him, despite the lingering bleak darkness held in check by the rain and the clouds overhead. It was unpleasant. But at least it was here and now. Solly had been pulled smack back into this cold, wet April morning by the wake of that strange and iniquitous vehicle driven by those two desperate men. He felt as if he were inextricably tied to them. And if not to them, at least to the forces that seemed to determine the fate of his friend Timothy.

He swiped at his face, took a long look back at the library and hurried on to Park Avenue and the tunnel at 40th Street.

There is something about New York City's midtown in the very early hours, in the rain, that sets it far apart from most other times...when the hordes, or even a moderate number of passersby fill her streets. She becomes yours. You share her quiet, her wide streets, her inhospitable coldness with no one. She leaves you a bitter taste, but you savor it. Because, to paraphrase Stephen Crane, it is bitter, and because it is yours. Only _you_ share the cold and damp with her and only _you_ watch her grow light. Only you have shared the intimacy of her lonliness, her darkness, her night. But soon, as the day drifts in with the slow but inevitable force of a blade of grass growing through a piece of concrete, she will give you up as another of her lost. And she will accommodate her onrushing crush of flotsam. For these are _her_ innards and she savors _them_ because they are hers. For the moment though, now, at 4 a.m. she swaddles _you_, and, for the moment, she is yours.

He did not know why, and, indeed, he had not stopped long enough to give it much thought, but Solly had been maintaining a quickened pace to reach the Park Avenue tunnel at 40th Street. From the corner at 90 Park Avenue, he dashed across half the street and then darted to his right, into the tunnel. Most of the lights were out inside and there was, as yet, no traffic jetting through. Leaning against the western wall Solly took another peek into Timothy's leather notebook. WALK ALONG THE CATWALK ON THE WEST SIDE OF THE TUNNEL, it said, amongst the other rather scribbled instructions on a page marked TUNNELS. Then it went on cryptically, YOU WILL FIND WHAT YOU ARE LOOKING FOR. USE WHAT YOU FIND AS YOU DID BEFORE. There were times, despite his intelligence, when Solly felt his confidence waning, particularly in situations where he could, for the moment, ostensibly make neither head nor tail of what was happening. Still, he thought, he would see it through. <u>That</u> was what had always saved him. <u>Seeing things through.</u> Most things anyway.

A couple of cars, preceded by blinding headlights, startled Solly as they tore through the early morning and this insignificant bit of city bowel. He hastened along the walk, not knowing what he was looking for. And then he saw it.

There, on the stone wall alongside the catwalk, was a narrow door. It was somewhat lower than what you would expect of a doorway in such a place, and was fairly inconspicuous save for one unique feature. Solly felt sure this <u>was</u> what he was 'looking' for. Behind some clumsy and rusted ladder arrangement leading to another level above this one, on the door itself was a little lion's head with a brass knocker held between its teeth. Solly took hold of it and let it go with one rap, then another. His chattering teeth might have made about as much noise. But the little door only concealed, apparently, a very small room. And it did not take long for the occupant of the room to respond to the alarm.

"Well, good morning," said Dr. Berg, not looking especially worn for that hour of the morning. "Do come in, young man. Do, by all means, come in."

The room was no more than a storage closet of ample size. Inside, a pull chain lamp hung from overhead, barely illuminating a dozen or so dust covered road signs, a few kerosene lanterns, broken glass, stacks of orange colored rubber traffic cones, a mop, pieces of pipe, an aluminum ladder, rags, paint cans, what looked like a bus seat, a flat tire, an army cot and a stool with a wicker top. "Sit down. Make yourself at home said Dr. Berg." He gestured hospitably toward the stool. Solly sat.

"I don't even know why I'm at this place...at this hour," Solly said, half to himself, shaking his head, "but Timothy asked that I come to see you. It happened all so quickly. I'm not even sure it <u>did</u> happen."

"What happened?" Dr. Berg looked comfortable enough, leaning back on the broken bus seat, smoking his pipe. In a way his aspect was consoling.

"Timothy was...arrested or something. A couple of men, dressed strangely, pulled up in an old model car, got out and apprehended him. They seemed to be after us both. In fact they assaulted us both for no apparent reason as we were coming down the steps of the 42nd Street Library. I managed to get away propelled by Timothy's exhortations to flee south to the tunnel. I inferred from him that I might find something of value here." After his ordeal Solly was waxing a bit sarcastic. "In any event, I couldn't very well hang around the library." He was beginning to recapture some of his breath but his face still dripped the combination of rain and perspiration. He paused and fixed Dr. Berg with a look that seemed to ask: 'Will this be of any value?'

"Was the automobile a Plymouth? Could it have been a 1946 Plymouth?"

"Why yes, it was. But how did you know?"

"Were both men in their forties? Dressed a little peculiarly?"

"You couldn't have been there?" Solly looked at Dr. Berg a trifle suspiciously. "Could you?"

"No," answered Dr. Berg. Then he added strangely, "not really."

"Then how could you have known?"

"Because," answered Dr. Berg, and he let out a long sigh, "I suppose things are going according to schedule." Then he looked up sharply at Solly. "Did Timothy get a chance to tell you about parallel events in time? Significant events recurring in separate time zones?"

"We touched on it to some extent. I'm not sure I fully understood..."

"Never mind. We'll go over it...in time." Dr. Berg gave the hint of a mischievous smile. "Meanwhile, what were you doing on the steps of the 42nd Street Library, at that hour?"

"We had gone for a walk. Timothy thought it might be a good place to talk. We talked a bit about you, in fact. But why do I think you already know that?" Solly suddenly realized why Dr. Berg's presence had seemed to mollify him. It was knowledge. Foreknowledge. The man exuded knowledge. He already had a grasp on what had happened. "But what in the world are you doing in this place, anyway? And, if I might add, at this hour?"

"Waiting for you, of course. I had had hopes of seeing Timothy along with you, but this turn of events does not come as a complete surprise. If things had gone according to our best scenario, we were all to have met here this morning."

Solly's heart took one of those skips which occur too quickly to control. It caused the unsteady, anxiety laced, sensation that indicates all is not well right now. "You mean this is our worst scenario?"

"This is not our best scenario."

"What happened?" Solly stood frozen in his anxieties. They seemed finally, this morning, to be catching up with him. Still, he had tenuous hopes of gaining some enlightenment through Dr. Berg. Certainly, he thought, if not through Berg, who else? Also, Dr. Berg did not seem terribly distraught. Nor did he seem surprised. Something might have been under control after all.

Berg puffed on his Bjarne. "These men. Was one of them on the lean side, dark and about five feet eight or nine inches tall? Did he have a round face with thinning hair on top?"

"Yes. But he was bald on top. Or very nearly."

"Of course. Of course. That would stand to reason.

<u>That,</u> my good fellow, was the infamous Mr. Gomez. I hope you got as good a look at him as your rather accurate description would indicate. You will be running into Mr. Gomez forthwith."

Solly chose to ignore Dr. Berg's prognostication for the moment. "What about Timothy? Is he all right? Where did they take him?" There seemed to be too many questions to ask and Dr. Berg was not quick at getting to the point of any of them. Rather he was far better at dodging inquiries, or, at least, creating more questions with his answers. Solly did not wish to continue the game. Still, few options remained.

"You will see Timothy again," said Dr. Berg, confidently. "I can promise you that. But you must do what I instruct. Much thought has preceded it. Much is at stake."

Solly's interest was peaked again. And Dr. Berg's tone was more benevolent than antagonizing. Moreover, it was apparent to Solly that Dr. Berg, more than anyone, possessed the keys...the answers to the elusive little mysteries that were entangling him more than he cared. "I don't wish to appear facetious," said Solly from what he felt was as good a starting point as any, "but what year is this?" It had occured to him he just might be in another time zone, through whatever means, and for whatever purpose.

Dr. Berg did not hesitate in giving his answer. "Your year," he said.

"Why me?" shot back Solly. "I think this is really what I want to know."

"Because," Dr. Berg looked Solly straight in one eye, "this is your time. Right place, right time! We can't change anything in the past. What is done, is done." Dr. Berg paused to smile. "Yes, the old cliches are true. We can alter the future, but we have to do it now."

"But what about Timothy dealing with that Senator? The one with the ID card? Wasn't that something that had been done in the past?"

"Not quite. We knew what she <u>was going</u> to do, and what it was going to lead to. We saw it in my scanner. But we saw it <u>then</u>! <u>Before</u> it was to have happened! And that's when we stopped it. THERE AND THEN! Had she gone ahead, and had she been allowed to succeed, it would indeed have been too late. We could not have gone <u>back</u> to stop her. It would have been too late. There would have been nothing anyone could have done."

"Wait a moment. Timothy told me I carried the card...right here in my wallet."

"That is correct," nodded Dr. Berg. "You see, Solly, you, the you who carried that card, were part of the future. And we saw that future. It was one possible existing future. But thanks to what we did, <u>that</u> future, the card, and a few of its nasty byproducts no longer exist...anywhere! Anytime! They are no longer a possibility. That's why you don't have the card or the recollection. Because even though that part of you once was, you no longer are, nor can you possibly be."

"Let me see if I clearly understand this. you're saying you can change the future... from the past. But you cannot change the past from the future."

"So far, so good."

"Can you change the present?"

"Relatively speaking you can always change the present. The present, if you can latch on to her, because she's an elusive devil, is the root of all change. And don't forget, the present was, at one time, a possible future. Now your man Gomez is sowing an attitude, an obsession, a commitment which is potentially destructive. Well, more than potentially. We have already seen where he's headed. We already know what he will eventually initiate. What he will personally instigate. In fact, we know more than he does. So far, Gomez only feels it, thinks it, and dreams it. He hasn't dared do anything, yet. He is like the female arachnid bearing her sack. He can't hatch his sack yet. Because it is not yet time. And you are going to ensure that that time does not arrive for Mr. Gomez. In other words, you are going to clean his clock...literally!"

'He took his vorpal sword in hand; long time the manxome foe he sought....'

Solly had lapsed for a moment.

"Clean his clock? But how?"

"That will be up to you, Solly. But I can tell you one thing. Have you ever seen a spider's sack break...when, let us say, you accidentally or intentionally stepped on one? The little ones are everywhere at once. Every which way! And if you're too close, they're all over **you...before...before** you know it. It's got to be a clean job. Fast. Clean. Not traceable."

"I still don't know how I'm ever going to do this."

"You're going to do it. We saw you do it! You made it work."

"I don't think so." But Solly was beginning to feel a strange headiness.

"Natural as pie."

"Really, I don't even know the man."

"You will. And he will know you. I can only promise you this, Solly. And it's a wonderful promise. You <u>will</u> succeed...if you undertake the matter with seriousness and sincerity. Don't falter. Do not turn back.

Do not question what you are doing. Believe in yourself, Solly. All resides within the self. You will succeed. We will all succeed."

"You were going to tell me why I was chosen to make this...this rendezvous."

Dr. Berg stood up and brushed at his slightly dusty trousers. He sauntered over toward an old STOP sign on which his suit jacket hung and began looking through the pockets as he spoke. "Because, Solly, you were the one whom I saw on the scanner. I saw **you** with Gomez. If you like, I'll show you what I saw."

Solly felt an amazing and near paralyzing thrill of anticipation. He hadn't felt so excited since he stood on 42nd Street peering into the night and the awninged windows of the Bristol. Dr. Berg took out a small blue velvet bag from his inside jacket pocket. A small penlike object was clipped to its side. Dr. Berg carefully removed the pen, then he gently emptied the contents of the bag onto his palm. It was a perfectly cut, smooth piece of luciteplexiglass, about four inches square. He held the pen to the glass plate.

"It's a kind of reflective surface, like a screen." Dr. Berg could not help but notice, not without pride, Solly's complete fascination Timothy, Dr. Berg was quite sure, had told Solly something of the basics of the device.

"It looks like a hologram." Solly was staring at the glass. His intense glance was fixed. At first he could see straight through it to the filthy floor below. Then he heard an audible click as he noticed the tiny movement of Dr. Berg's thumb turning the pen on. Instantly Solly could make out confused images in the little slab. At first it seemed like one image kept turning and changing. Then he saw it. There were <u>several</u> images. And they <u>were</u> turning and changing. It was like a movie, going on inside this lucite plate.

"Now watch." Dr. Berg turned one of the half dozen dials on the pen. The images within the lucite changed in both shape and color. Each set of images seemed superimposed on another set. And each set was set apart by virtue of its being bathed in an aura of its own, unique, dominating color. Each color group comprised countless variations of tone and minute shadings. "This dial is for tuning," said the Doctor. It brings in our signals. It behaves like an F-Stop on a 35mm camera. The more I open it up, the more receptive it is to the weaker, more distant signals, namely those from further and further into the future."

"Can we tune in on the past, as well?"

"The past is another pen entirely," answered Dr. Berg with the smug satisfaction of one who had not only anticipated the question but the answer as well. "It has a separate set of receptors for a much stronger signal, that signal already having occurred." Solly was still peering into the glass. "You see," Dr. Berg continued, "all our yesterdays are still very much with us: reverberating, echoing, afterimaging, lingering, all over the place, much more, of course, than our tomorrows. But the future is a much less definite business, and often no more than a blur because of its many possibilities. Still, one outcome of events usually does stand out through a set of far cleaner, stronger signals. It is this outcome toward which favorable statistics naturally gravitate; it is this event which we can tune in on; and it is this possible occurrence on which you can safely bet your money...unless, of course, somebody or something runs interference."

"Why are these images different colors? I've never seen such strange colors."

"The colors indicate the nature of an event, its intensity, in terms of distance in time, its magnitude, and its significance. Blue generally denotes distance and weakness. Usually, although there are exceptions, as we draw closer in time or intensity, the colors appear to be warmer. In any case, the eye is unable to discern with more than the most general accuracy what degree of colors are being received. We run them through a complete spectrum analysis. The degrees of variation would amaze you. The relationship between the colors are important also. See, here, these two islands of color do not seem to go together by any stretch of the imagination. They simply do not mix. The events they represent, indeed those we can actually see by fine tuning our shapes and forms, are completely unrelated and have no effect on one another. This is quite rare and would be because of great time or space barriers. Or perhaps because one event was completely obliterated prior to the emergence of the second event. But let me show you something that has already happened. Something already borne out by history."

Dr. Berg reached into his shirt pocket and took out another pen. This one had a gold rather than a silver cap. He paused to study one of the moving hologramlike clouds that appeared in the glass as he removed the cap from the pen and, without looking, turned one of its dials counterclockwise. He was like a biologist examining a slide through a microscope. Then Dr. Berg turned his attention to the gold capped pen. He spoke as he continued to make a series of increasingly fine adjustments on the delicate instrument.

"In the late 1800's a man named Mansfield wrote a novel about a marvelous ocean liner, an Atlantic ocean liner. It was the largest of its kind ever built." Dr. Berg glanced at his slide again, then back at the pen. He continued his story, slowly. "According to the novel, the ship sailed far out into the Atlantic with a rather impressive list of wealthy and well known passengers, but too few lifeboats. The inevitable happened. The ship struck an iceberg and went down. Mansfield called his ill fated ship the **TITAN.** Some years later, you may recall, another doomed vessel shared a similar fate. Ironically, it had almost the same name...**the TITANIC**. Now look here," he directed, "<u>This</u> and <u>this</u> show something else. Do you see the same forms, the same brown hue over both groups? See how one seems to have come out of the other?"

Solly could see a connection between the two wisps Dr. Berg was referring to. At first he thought it was one image. But they were somewhat apart, one nearly superimposed above the other.

"Let me enhance this for you." The doctor moved two more dials on his pen which he aimed at the brown wisps. The top of the pen opened slightly. Tiny forms began to take shape in the glass. "There won't be any sound, of course. There can be, but it needs too much reconstitution. Not worth the bother. I'm tuning in to something that happened in 1943. A peculiar event, little known today, but one which could have had great significance. One which could have, in fact, changed the course of history. It's taken me quite some time to locate these exact coordinates but what you're seeing is more or less an unrefined essense of what took place on that fateful November day. Let me explain."

There was something hypnotic in Dr. Berg's intonation. That, coupled with the fascination of the forms on the hand held plexiglass plates riveted Solly's focus.

"President Roosevelt along with several top ranking generals and admirals was en route to the Cairo Conference where Roosevelt was to meet with Churchill and Chiang Kaishek. They were crossing the Atlantic on the battleship Iowa. Some 350 miles off the island of Bermuda, a nearby destroyer, one of ours, which had been conducting routine exercises fired a torpedo at the Iowa. The torpedo was thought to have been unarmed. It was not. The Iowa tried to turn out of the torpedo's path. But the torpedo was detonated by the turbulence, and exploded in the Iowa's wake.

It was very close. A few seconds, a few feet, could have made all the difference. Had she hit, had the Iowa gone down with the cream of America's strategists and leadership aboard, destiny, there and then, would indeed have been altered."

Solly looked into the plate. The effect of the blurry brown cloud taking shape was hypnotic. He could, he thought, make out tiny shapes of vessels and water. What's more, he could feel the event and its nearly catastrophic significance as Dr. Berg related the tale. Suddenly there was a beautifully brilliant blast, or so it seemed, followed by a tranquil blue field within the lucite. When the numbing shock that came with the realization of what could have been wrought by such a careless mistake subsided, Solly was engulfed by a feeling of well being and a hope he knew would be realized. He saw the Iowa taking the President and his entourage to Cairo and toward the end of the war. He saw a golden sun set on that fateful day as guided by a benevolent hand and spirit. And there prevailed for him, for the moment, a serene feeling which seemed to convey to Solly all the good and the pride he had ever felt about his country. "You see," said Dr Berg, "it seems to affect one on all possible levels, events like this. Visual signals are not the only ones received by the pen and reflected by the screen. But something in here disturbs me." Dr. Berg pointed to the second brownish mass on the plate. "See, it is reforming again. It's the Iowa again, yet it seems to be in another place...another time. Still, it's the same ship, clouded over by those same somber tones, as if it can't seem to shake its fate. Something is going to happen aboard her again, another close call of tragic proportions, only I don't know when. And I'm afraid finding out would be a needle in a haystack job. I suppose it's something we just have to accept. Some things in this world travel through time under a dark cloud." He lit his pipe again, it had gone out long ago, and motioned to Solly. "Come on," he said, follow me. I want to introduce you to Mr. Gomez."

CROSSROADS

As the 1946 Plymouth cut its wheels to skid around a sharp 39th Street corner on its way west, Timothy could feel a slight nausea evolving from within. The combined smells of the cloth upholstery of the car and its Bakelite dash and trim was not altogether unpleasant but, in filling his nostrils, it seemed to bring about a vague déjà vu which was reinforced by everything in the car, including its two rather unsavory and heavyhanded passengers. And the possibility that he might have experienced such an unsettling and threatening encounter before, or at least at some other time, was enough to leave him with a sickly feeling.

Flashes of city light sliced through the little side windows of the black sedan as it raced past neon night signs along the side streets. They were instant indicators to Timothy that something was very wrong. Neon signs at this early hour should long have been dark. It wasn't a moment later that the hurrying sedan drew the attentions of the occupants of an inconspicuously parked New York City squad car. But as it pulled out smartly behind the Plymouth, Timothy observed the police car was not blue and white. It was green and black. Indeed, it suddenly became clear to him that not only was the hour earlier, so apparently was the year.

When the driver of the sedan became aware of the squad car on his tail he darted straight ahead for Broadway and careened around the corner just south of Times Square to head uptown through what had suddenly, it seemed to Timothy, become crowded, noisy streets, with blaring lights and activity. The police car threw its high beams on, signaling the sedan to stop. The sedan ignored the bright lights and continued to wend, wildly through the traffic. An all embracing confusion enveloped Timothy who was desperately trying to keep hold of his powers of reason. Failure, he knew, to think this through, would inevitably end in disaster. He shut his eyes momentarily. Where was he? Where had he just been? He recalled Solly and the Library. But, somehow, 1946 seemed so fresh and vivid in his recollection. He opened his eyes and peered through the side windows of the Plymouth. There they were, the giant lights and billboards of Times Square, not as he remembered them, but as he knew them to be...now! CHEVROLET, CAPITOL THEATER, PLANTER'S PEANUTS, THE CRITERION, THE ASTOR and THE AUTOMAT. There was HECTOR'S CAFETERIA, the giant sign for KLEENEX, trolley cars, and directly above and in front of him, a rather appealing, refreshing looking, neon glass of **RUPPERT BEER.** He wished he could **'MAKE IT MINE'** as the billboard suggested. The car swung left on 45th Street and shot toward the West Side Highway. Timothy realized it wasn't simply the hypnotic call of the Great White Way lights that brought the year to life for him. He had just been reading, that very day it seemed, about Walter Reuther, the new president of the United Auto Workers. And about the steel strikes, the coal strikes and the rail strikes. The great names were fresh in his mind. Joe Louis knocking out Billy Conn, Ernest Hemingway getting married again...for a fourth time. Ted Williams had just hit a trio of homeruns in the All Star Game, and he had just seen, or so it seemed, John Garfield and Lana Turner together in The Postman Always Rings Twice. Then there were the places that were 1946 standing out in bold relief. Palestine. Nuremberg. Bikini Lagoon: The Zionist terrorists. The Nazi trials. The Atomic bomb test. Timothy's head was spinning. The notion that it might <u>not</u> be 1946 and that he had indeed just stepped out of the 1980's was fast fading. Asking the man at his side if he could reach for his handkerchief, he felt inside his jacket pocket. There was his pipe, a pouch of Half and Half tobacco, an all white handkerchief, and a few nickels. They were mostly Indian Head, Buffalo nickels. All the better to ride the subways and buses with, thought Timothy. None of the coins in any of his pockets was dated beyond 1945. He was gathering his wits, however scattered they were. Parts of an incident that had nightmarish overtones were beginning to come together. Timothy addressed the driver.

"Where are you taking me?" Somehow he was less than surprised when no answer was forthcoming. "Would someone mind telling me what this is about?" The car was now careening wildly in an effort to further elude the pursuing squad car which was momentarily stuck behind a bottling company truck. A siren could be heard in the distance. The man sitting beside Timothy grinned stupidly at him.

"People like you have long noses," he said. "You don't mind your business. You worry about what doesn't concern you. So we're going to fix things for you. Soon you won't have anything to worry about." His grin never left his face. His eyes never left Timothy's face.

Timothy knew he had seen the man before. Of course. He worked for Gomez. He had seen him many times before with Gomez. Only he had never heard him speak. And the driver! Could it be? He had been unable to get a good look at the driver's face because of the light, his position and the overall confusion. And the man himself was keeping well covered. He seemed to enjoy a special rapport with the shadows. But, Timothy asked himself, when was it that he had become so familiar with these two? Then, suddenly, just as the decades had seemed moments ago to mesh all at once, as the car screeched onto the West Side Highway heading South, several things became clear to Timothy. First, he had come to know both these men sometime recently. Second, somehow <u>they</u> were unaware of any change in time. They may have <u>nabbed</u> Timothy out of the eighties, but they themselves never really left the forties. Third, something terrible was about to happen. "Gomez!" Timothy shouted. The driver, unperturbed by the outburst, glanced up to view Timothy's face in the rear view mirror. Timothy looked squarely into the mirror and knew. It <u>was</u> Gomez! There was no doubt in his reflection. Timothy thought Gomez must also have spotted the police squad car in the mirror because he punctuated his glance by flooring the accelerator. The car's wheels skidded briefly on the wet cobblestones of the drive.

The confusion brought about by the apparent variation of time was diminishing, and in its place Timothy was beginning to feel a strong need to do something about the present crisis. For the moment, the year of his dilemma did not matter to him. It was the immediacy of his situation from which he had to flee. 1943. There was something significant about 1943. Just as he sat, ever so precariously and dangerously in 1946, could he possibly find himself in 1943? Why not? He didn't have to be dragged like he just had been. Possibly it could be done. Certainly, it had to be. Timothy knew otherwise he would not live through this night.

The sign on the side of the wet road read: SLOW 15 MPH. The Plymouth was about to go around a sharp curve. Timothy knew of something called **SYNCHRONICITY.** It was the coincidence in time of two or more cauSolly unrelated events which have the same or similar meaning. He had the uncomfortable but distinct feeling that something terrible, that <u>had</u> happened to him before, was about to happen again, he knew it was imminent but he knew of something referred to by followers of Carl Jung as "the Gambler's Principle". And he was going to use it.

The "Gambler's Principle" stated that on the point of death or disaster all energies are focused on the turn, the <u>final</u> turn, of a card...or event. If one's mental powers are such that all one's energies can be concentrated on that final turn, if one risks <u>everything</u> on that final play, psychic energies will do the rest. Synchronicities are bound to occur, that is, that one chance in a million, that impossible long shot. But the principle had to be approached carefully. One doubt, one misstep and he would be gone. There would be no infusion of energies and the turn would not respond favorably. But it could be almost like taking Solly into the Library, or out of the Rackets, but Timothy was taking himself, and his life depended on it. And, as the great comics say, timing was everything.

Indestructible energy. Timothy thought, indestructible energy. He had it. He was riding on it. He was going to take it with him. 1943. He must think 1943. He began a stream of consciousness rooted in 1943. **The war. The OPA. The closing of the Office of War Information.**

New Georgia. The Marines landing on the island of New Georgia. Messina. The Flying Fortresses. The Army Air Corps, Martinique. The dark Caribbean nights. Enemy U-Boats. The black outs. The air raids. The Air Raid Wardens. The Plymouth began skidding around the sharp curves. **Names. Hull. Cordell Hull. Secretary of the Treasury Henry Morganthau. Grumman. Grumman F6F Hellcat Fighters. Stimson, Biddle, Farley, Forrestal, Wallace. Pope Pius XII. Tony Zale, Willie Pep and the Brown Bomber. Sid Luckman of the Chicago Bears, Center Clyde Bulldog Turner.** The car was going faster. It was skidding. Gomez hit the brake. The Plymouth started spinning. **Faster. The Derby winner. The Preakness winner. Winner of the Belmont. Count Fleet.** With every name, every idea, there was picture, a sensation, eidetic imagery that infused Timothy's every fibre. **Cars. All black cars. Hudsons, Desotos. Nashes. Packards. The Three Caballeros. Kate Smith. God Bless America and Ice cream Parlors.** He was gathering momentum. Acceleration. The thoughts were coming faster and faster. As if each were giving rise to three... four More. **Frankie. The bow ties. The bobby sox. The saddle shoes. Sinatra. 4F...again. Ration books and tokens. Saturday Evening Post. Heroes. Joe Foss. Red Cross and the USO. Ernie Pyle. Jalopys. Roy Rogers, Fedoras and Doris Day. Rosie the Riviter, Joe Palooka and Sad Sack.** He was feeling heady. It was as if he couldn't stop. He couldn't think of any other time. He was caught up by it. In it. **The Trib, the Mirror and the World Telegram & Sun. The Bond Drive Posters and the shipyards. Victory Gardens and Paper Drives. Metal toothpaste tubes, rubber scrap, cans of bacon grease. WACS, Ann Sheridan, Rita Hayworth. Olive drab subway cars. West Side Diners.** He saw a newsy selling a Times for three cents. He bought it and heard the newsy's **Emerson** say 'the following program will be interupted for any important war bulletins'. He saw an old wood and glass telephone booth and read the exchanges from the phone book inside: **Columbus, Rhinelander, Melrose, Susquehanna,**

Butterfield, Pennsylvania, Circle, Plaza. He saw the different neighborhoods that sat behind and worked behind and answered the phones of those exchanges: the business world downtown of **Judson and Yukon,** to the more residential **Ludlows, Murray Hills, and Wadsworths.** The street lights were sodium vapor dimmer. In the distance, behind him there was the immense span of the George Washington Bridge. Across the river was **Bill Miller's Riviera** in Fort Lee. Saturday night fare, as were the women in long hair, trolley cars, the **Satuday Post** with **Oaky Doaks** and **Dickie Dare.** He thumbed through the paper under the high, yellow glowing, street lamp. Stories of the **Seige of Leningrad...broken. Roosevelt and Churchill hold their ten day war summit in Casablanca. MaCarthur vows to retake the Phillipines. U.S. Bombers hit bases in the Solomons.**

The Plymouth skids, strikes the guard rail and, to the wail of a police siren closeby, goes plummeting down into the Hudson below. Somehow though, for a long moment, it seems to hover there. Timothy's mind is a blur of images. **Allies take Tunisia. The war in Africa is over. Invasion of Sicily begins. Stalin, Roosevelt and Churchill attend the Teheran conference. Chiang Kai-shek attends the Cairo Conference. Italy surrenders and Mussolini is hanged. Thousands die on the beaches of Tarawa. Marines move through Bouganville as they prepare their assault on Rabaul. Red Army moves on the Black Sea and crushing thousands of German troops in the squeeze. Crimea is sealed off and the Russians smash Nazi resistance. General Eisenhower is named Allied Invasion Commander. There is the smell of victory in the air.**

Timothy no longer knew exactly where he was. He had got totally engulfed in what he had been doing and, in fact, was no longer conscious at all that he was doing it. The names, places and circumstances, the events, were beyond flood stage and were rushing, unstoppable, in torrents into and about the vicinity of Timothy's psyche and very being.

He felt himself submerged, swallowed up into the world of 1943. And from somewhere, he could hear **Bill Stern** weave his tales of heroic sports figures that may or may not have existed, and **Roma Wines** bringing you **Suspense.** The city, he thought to himself, is a film noir. Then, from nowhere in particular, a doleful voice seemed to be admonishing him: 'whatever you do, **Don't Sit Under The Apple Tree With Anyone Else But me'.**

Just before the 1946 Plymouth Sedan plunged onto the rocks of the river below the West Side Highway, Timothy recalled part of the opening to an old radio program called Grand Central Station: **'As a bullet seeks its target. shining rails in every part of our great country are aimed at Grand Central Station, heart of the nation's greatest city. Drawn by the magnetic force of the fantastic metropolis, day and night great trains rush toward the Hudson River, sweep down its Eastern bank for 140 miles, flash briefly by the long, red row of tenement houses South of 110th Street, dive with a roar into the two and a half mile tunnel which burrows beneath the glitter and swank of Park Avenue, and then...Grand Central Station, crossroads of a million lives...gigantic stage, on which are played a thousand dreams daily.'**

But, oddly, his last thought that night in 1946 was of a crowd of young servicemen at Pennsylvania Station on New York's West Side.

CHEMERA

Dr. Berg stood up and motioned for Solly to follow. Reaching a sidewall in the little room, which seemed only to serve as a support for the worn and discarded New York City props long turned to clutter and dust casts, the stocky little man shoved, more than slid, the entire panel to his left. It revealed another room. "You like movies," he asked? Dr. Berg turned on a light and they both stepped inside, avoiding the debris scattered about the floor.

"Why have you picked a place like this to...to entertain?" asked Solly. Apparently he had felt the need to seize the vacant moment and inject it with a dose, however small, of levity. Dr. Berg seemed immune.

"Can you think of a better place?" answered Dr. Berg."No one ever comes here, certainly not at this hour. Besides," he muttered, "it appeals to my cryptic side." As Solly wondered what side that might be, Dr. Berg unrolled a small screen and flicked on a 16mm projector. The image of a familiar face captured Solly's attention as a whirring noise filled the small room.

"Let me tell you a little about our Mr. Raymond Gomez," began Dr. Berg. "He works in this bank. A merger of two banks, actually. It was initially known as the Chemerican, but has since shortened its name to Chemera. Appropriate somehow, I think. Here's Gomez at his desk at the 33rd Street branch. He's giving a customer a bad time. You might notice, through his rigid expression, he has absolutely no sense of humor and takes himself and his purposes, inextricably intertwined, quite seriously." The film purred on, the players using animated gestures to make their points. The man at the desk, however, for the most part seemed cold and unresponsive. "Gomez actively seeks, to establish no rapport with anyone, seems to be at cross purposes with everyone, and will never yield or back down on <u>any</u> point of contention, especially if it can cause someone inconvenience or embarrassment. He is not of a persuasion which might be characterized as reasonable. That is to say, he is not swayed by good, verbal, logical argument. And he is certainly not what you would call a nice guy." Suddenly Solly knew where he had seen the man, Gomez.

"That's the character we ran into on the steps of the Library!"

"Yes, I am aware."

Solly recalled Dr. Berg had indicated this earlier but seeing the mysterious Gomez as indeed the same brute who had assaulted him and Timothy only an hour or so before was unsettling. "He seems very adamant in his argument with this customer," Solly observed, although there was no sound to the film.

"Yes," agreed Dr. Berg. "He is completely unmoved by this man's dilemma. He will doggedly pursue his own ends, embracing any chance at power along the way. No measure of dialogue nor attempt at persuasion on the victim's part will work. Gomez is extremely selfrighteous and any form of bribery or patronage will only cement his resolve." The man in the movie who had been presenting his case before Gomez bowed his head and turned away, clutching the few slips of paper he apparently had hoped would win his case. Gomez scrawled something on a form and placed it into his desk drawer, which he shut and locked. "Gomez is driven, obsessive and ruthless. And," said Dr. Berg, gesturing toward the screen, "once he has your name on paper he will never give it up. He is the consummate collector. He will not surrender one piece in his collection. To do so would be to break the chain of power, to release his hold, to allow a chink in his armor, a leak in his system. He would rather die." The clip ended abruptly, there was a rush of leader, and shadows of scratches and smudges danced across the screen."Gomez doesn't especially sound like anyone I'm particularly keen on meeting, added Solly." The fact that he somehow felt compelled to use understatement did not strike Solly as amusing. What he wanted really was to go home to a pleasant, warm bed and sleep all of this away. Dr. Berg flicked the lights back on.

"I know you don't want to meet Gomez, Solly. But you already have. We can only hope now, this will be the last time."

"So where do I go? What do I do?" The phrases carried with them some resignation.

"On the corner of 33rd Street and Eighth Avenue, across the street from where the old Penn Station used to be," said Dr. Berg, "is the Chemera Bank. It opens in just a little while. And so far as you, and our purposes, are concerned, there's no point waiting beyond today. Timothy gave you some bills?"

"Yes." Solly checked the leather book. The bills were inside. There were fifties and hundreds.

"The bills are not real. You will present them to Gomez to be deposited in an account which is not yours, although you will have the passbook. Here it is." Dr. Berg handed Solly a neat, but somewhat aged passbook. It was crinkled, stamped in different colored inks, and stained. It looked like one of those hastily written, distressed diaries customized for the IRS to substantiate tax deductions. "It's under Timothy's name. Gomez will spot the bills and he isn't going to like the passbook not being yours. Fight him as best you can. But goad him. Bait him. Let him close around you like a squid. He is sure to do that by virtue of your simply being as innocent and as civil as you can. The more you seem victimized, the harder he will work to ensnare you. Remember, you cannot enlist his sympathies. He has none. But the more you try to win him over, the more you will succeed in antagonizing him...which is what we want. Tell him you will take him to the party who gave you the bills. Make a show of trying to convince him to make a deal. He won't go for it. His reasoning will not extend beyond the lure of catching you at the bribe he will sense. He will attempt to detain you, or he will let you slip away, only to pursue you. But lure him out. Lead him to Pennsylvania Station.

And leave him there. You have but to cross the street. Remember that...and think of nothing else. It <u>will</u> work."

"How do I get <u>back</u>?"

"Same way you left. Just cross the street and walk back into the bank. They won't know you anymore. Turn around and walk out...like you have just walked into the wrong bank."

"It's preposterous that this can actually work...and yet...." Solly knew he had seen it work last night. At least he <u>thought</u> he knew. "By the way, what year, may I ask, are we headed for?"

"Good question. And I'm glad you asked. Circa 1943. But don't think too much about it. Just do it. It'll happen."

"I wish I had your confidence. Still, I don't fully understand this modus operandi, I'm afraid."

"Did you ever hear of something called ISOSPIN?"

"It has to do with subparticle movement, doesn't it?"

"Not exacly. But close. You see, although a proton is said to have 'spin' it really does not 'spin' but performs something analogous to 'spin'. In effect, the proton's mathematical wave function changes in a way that can be likened to the mathematical changes in a spinning object as we know it. But that is only the beginning. ISOSPIN is a second type of spin engaged in by the proton. But it does not take place in the <u>space</u> with which we are familiar. ISOSPIN occurs in a kind of abstract space called **ISOSPACE.** So, in the first case, the proton, which has virtually no spatial dimensions, has 'spin' without spinning, and in the second case, it spins without spinning in space as we know it. Most likely, <u>that</u> is how the Cheshire Cat pulled off its appearing and disappearing stunts. The point is, just as one proton can 'spin' into ISOSPACE, so can a collection of particles follow on the same track. It's governed by the same force. The same principal. <u>That</u> principle makes it possible. And, knowing it is possible, we do it!" Dr. Berg gave a little Cheshire smile, himself. "You see, Solly, ultimately there is no distinction between the mental and the material. It is all one, governed by one central determining principle. Carl Jung noted that one can, through lucid dreaming, actually draw correct time-space coordinates and travel to past realms. Timothy took you to the old Croton Reservoir, didn't he? Well, you see, you had been there before! We all were! But Timothy knew how to get there again! His genius lies in his vivid memory. Almost total recall, Proustian, and the ability to form unbroken associative chains with highly unique and original, almost indetectible, links at great rapidity. It stems, mostly, from Timothy's ability to observe and retain, and recall, of course, great stores of detail. He doesn't have to think about it, so there is no intermediary process to slow the images down. No room for doubt. Everything is simply there, and automatically flows. His resulting onrush of recalled images, perceptions and events nearly imitates life itself! And, subtle though the connections may be, all the bits of information are intertwined. The result is a virtual re-creation in Timothy's mind, and for all his senses, of what has actually occurred. There is a re-creation of events. A re-creation of that very year. Timothy melts into the year; the year envelopes Timothy. The two merge. **It's like a snake swallowing its tail...and vanishing!"** Dr. Berg reached over to Solly and took the small leather notebook from his hands. He flipped through the back pages. They were filled with numbers, letters and signs. "But, some of us have an advantage," he continued. "Timothy was a walking store of coordinates. He has some of them listed here. He knew the time-space coordinates linked to events, years, decades, that most would be hard pressed to memorize, not to mention understand. But Timothy more than just memorized them, he **knew** them! It was as if he were tapping his collective unconscious. As if he were lucid dreaming selectively while awake. Still, that is not always necessary. Timothy liked to combine his natural gifts with more pragmatic efforts. But there are some few of us who can move by instinct alone. We can travel through belief and trust. You are one such individual, Solly. You have shown us that already. The library was a test. So was The Rackets. Not too many pass that one. They're all still hanging around **Mortimers,** wondering where everybody went!"

"You mean The Rackets isn't really there?"

"Oh, it's there, all right. But you have to be able to get to where it's at. But you did all right. You were tuned in."

Dawn was breaking outside. Solly could tell by the sounds of trucks roaring through the tunnel, the general and nearly sudden increase in traffic, and what he was only recently beginning to perceive: a very keen sense that he seemed to possess, of time and place. He did feel tuned in.

"But now," said Dr. Berg in a low tone, "now you will be on your own. Now, you will have no help." Dr. Berg handed Solly back the little leather notebook. "Don't forget about the bills," he said. "They're very important. And when you're finished come back to Mortimers. I'll be waiting for you." He put his pipe in his mouth and extended his hand. "Good luck."

Solly slipped out the narrow door as he had come in, unnoticed, and with no less anxiety about what lay ahead. He ran south along the catwalk until he reached the outside and that certain security that comes with being on the surface. Traffic was in full force, albeit that description's misnomer. That is to say, the cars, trucks and buses were gridlocked in every which way and not at all moving. There was a haze as far as one could, or could not, see, and things before his very eyes, especially in the wake of a rather nebulous night, did not appear to be in sharp focus.

He traveled west through the side streets of the thirties letting his surroundings, millenary shops, bead boutiques, fur vaults, snack counters and warehouses, punctuate his thoughts. At moments the street would seem to embrace him, however uncomfortably. He noticed, for example, the farther west he walked, the more people seemed deformed. And at the corner of Eighth and 33rd, there appeared more homeless and twisted than in New Dehli, India.

Then he saw it. CHEMERA BANK. It was, however, as if he had never really seen the words before. He stepped through the revolving doors, past the plainclothes guard, to the end of a long redrope bordered line, and joined the queue. A digital sign at the front of the line read: AVERAGE WAIT 3 MINUTES. Ten minutes later Solly was still waiting. He clutched Timothy's passbook between whose covers were folded several fifty and one hundred dollar bills. His hands were moist. The sign still flashed "3 minutes". His heart beat perceptibly. There were only two people before him now.

Across from the red rope, on the far side of the bank, were several desks, only two or three of which seemed occupied. Sometimes a bank officer would give up one desk for another, for an available form, to accommodate a customer, or to pick up a phone. One man in particular seemed to be at everyone's desk at once. Solly broke into a sweat for fear the officer would know him. For an instant the man looked up and glared directly at the line and their eyes met. But there was no glimmer of recognition. A teller called, "Next!"

Solly stepped out from the protective confines of the red rope and past the digital sign. He found the available teller and slid his documents before her, under a narrow slot, all the space which remained under a shield of impenetrable three inch thick lucite. She examined the one hundred dollar bill for a moment, asked Solly to wait and picked up a phone. Turning her head only slightly to the side, she made little effort at concealing the words "bill check" which Solly could hear even through the plexiglass shield. And it became obvious that the person on the other end of the phone was Gomez, who came running over from the the other end of the bank to get buzzed in. He looked at the bill, then at Solly whom he asked: "Do you have an account at this branch?"

"No, but I use this branch frequently."

"I'm sorry, but I'll have to confiscate this bill. Would you please step that way." He gestured toward his desk.

"Could I cash this check?" Solly removed a check that had been folded in Timothy's book along with the bills. He slipped it under the cage.

Gomez snatched it and scanned it quickly. "This can only be deposited."

"But it's made out to me. I have identification. There's enough in the account to cover it. Can't I just cash it?"

"This is income. It has to be deposited," countered Gomez. He was very sharp, to the point of being nasty.

"Never mind. Give me the check back. I'll take care of it elsewhere."

"If you don't mind I'd like to take a closer look at this check. If you would please step away from the teller and over to my desk, please."

"Would you give me back my deposit slip, and the check, and my money, please?"

"I'm sorry. I'm afraid that will not be possible. Step over to my desk." Gomez turned and left the teller's area. Solly followed him to his desk.

Gomez did not raise his head, picked up the phone, dialed two digits and spread the check out before him. He placed the bill in his drawer and filled out a small slip of paper which he handed to Solly. "This is your receipt," he mumbled. "Can you run a check on this number?" Gomez sliced into the receiver. Then he reeled off the account number digits on the face of the check and waited.

"It's <u>my</u> account," said Solly, leaning in toward Gomez, even though he was aware of the discrepancy between the names on his check and Timothy's passbook. It didn't seem to matter. Gomez pretended not to hear him.

"What are you trying to do, young man?" Gomez hung up the phone. "Transfering funds arbitrarily? Laundering bad money? What's your game?

I'm going to have to keep this check." He picked up the telephone again.

"Look. Just give me the check back. It's my check. And I don't think you can just indiscriminately take someone's check and appropriate it for no reason. I understand about the bill but I need the check for my records." Gomez was ignoring him. "Please give me my check back." Gomez continued dialing the two digits that were apparently busy. Solly reached for the check that lay on the desk. But he let Gomez grab it first.

"Security? Can you send a man down here? I think we may have a possible problem."

"Would you please let me leave with my check? It won't mean anything to you, but I need it for my records. There's nothing wrong with the check, I can assure you." Gomez feigned as if not hearing him. "It's the bills you should be concerned with. The bills are filtering through this branch!" Solly was on automatic pilot now. Gomez looked up.

"What did you say? What are you talking about?"

"These bills. Look. I got them from your machine today." Solly had had sudden inspiration. He reached into his jacket pocket and fished out a couple of fifties and hundreds.

"What machine? Where? Let me see those bills." Gomez reached to take hold of the bills. Solly drew his hand back.

"The machines across the street. These bills are coming straight from your machines. If you just give me back what's mine I'll show you what I'm talking about."

Gomez smiled at Solly. "First of all, our machines only dole out twenties. We don't use fifties and hundreds in the automatic tellers."

"How do you think I knew anything was unusual? I'm not a counterfeiter. The machine is just spitting them out."

"All right! Let's see what you're talking about."

"How about my check?"

"You'll get your check back when I see what you're talking about, young man." A security officer stepped forward from a stairwell and paced rapidly towards Gomez's desk.

"Everything all right?"

"Fine. Everything is fine, Lou. We'll be back in a few minutes." Gomez reached for his jacket which was draped around his swivel chair, locked his drawer, and with a large hand took hold of Solly's shoulder, squeezing it, nearly turning him in the direction of the bank's revolving door. "Okay. Let's go. Let's see what the hell you're talking about."

'He took his vorpal sword in hand...long time the manxome foe he sought....'

PENN STATION

In the bank's vestibule Gomez was still adjusting his jacket and hat when he stopped in his tracks. "Just what machine location are you referring to? I don't recall that we have anything in the immediate area other than what's right over here." His tone was cold and businesslike. He made no eye contact with Solly.

"Penn Station," Solly said. "Remember the old Penn Station? Well, there used to be an entire bank of night deposit boxes downstairs. They're not there now, of course, but the same area accommodates your money machines."

"You know," said Gomez, "I have the feeling you don't know what you're talking about. But you had best not be wasting my time. I think you're in trouble, young man."

"I assure you I know what I'm talking about." Solly revealed the bills once again. "Take a look at this." He extended a fifty and a one hundred dollar bill to Gomez, pointing at the date on each bill. Gomez snatched them.

"You realize I can't give these back to you."

"I understand," said Solly. "You've already made that clear." He was disarming Gomez and was quite aware of it. So to temper his patronage somewhat, he added "I can get more of them if I want."

"Not if I have a hand in it."

"But notice the dates. None of the bills are older than 1943." Solly had noticed the dates when he had observed the crisp texture and bright green coloring of the notes on his way to the bank. No wonder the teller was so quick to sense something different about the bills. Dr. Berg, for some reason, had said they weren't real, and Solly didn't exactly know what he had meant by that, because the currency seemed to be perfectly legitimate. Still, the color and texture of the old bills, especially in such, literally, mint condition as they appeared, was brighter and thicker than later currency and caused the notes to stand out, to say the least. Furthermore, some of the bills read **SILVER CERTIFICATE** while others, particularly the hundreds, bore bright red seals on their faces and read **UNITED STATES NOTE.** If the bills were not counterfeit they certainly were collector's items giving some indication, when casually passed, that something may have been afoul. "Remember 1943?"

"What?"

"1943. The year 1943. The war? You remember the war. All those hordes of guys in uniform. Soldiers. Sailors. Duffle bags. Seabags. Wives and girlfriends in kerchiefs and cloth coats, wide brimmed hats and high heels, kissing their men goodbye. They were all out there. Crowding into Pennsylvania Station. Down the marble stairs under the giant American flags onto the main concourse. Or down from between the Roman pillars and beneath the hanging Benrus clock at the 33rd Street entrance. And then down, down beneath the domes of sunlit glass, under the vaults and arches, through the wrought ironwork, steel ribs and grillwork, past the crisscross girders and seethrough pillars. And down, down along the clanging steel stairways from the 'open level above it to the great track level below."

"What are you talking about?"

"The money. That's where the money is. That's where it's coming from. All those new, crisp, rag paper, bills. That's where the machine is. You want it? Come on, I'll take you right to it!" Gomez did not hesitate. He followed Solly right out of the alcove. Right out into the sunlight of that Autumn day in 1943. Right out under the blue of another sky, a sky that'd come and gone and yet will always be, letting the light above and beyond it shine through, to illuminate and lend color to that sea of shoppers in polka-dotted dresses, the mix of uniforms from Navy blue to United States Marine Corps green, and the chests of ribbons and shining metal merit badges reflecting sharp glints of sun right into your eyes. The two men rushed across the street, one slightly behind the other, to the impressively massive, stately, block long, Romanesque edifice that was **Pennsylvania Station.**

The cars that were rushing by were black except for the taxicabs. Some of those were actually checkered, and some were checkered green and white. All the vehicles were rounder. The buses and busstop signs were rounder. The people appeared rounder. The day seemed rounder. There was a softness in the air that seemed to lend shape to the day itself. There were flags and stars in windows and there were bond drive posters pasted on lamp posts. Gomez peered through the haze only for a moment before quickening his pace to keep up with Solly. They dashed up the few stairs past several pairs of legs in seamed stockings as well as those in baggy cuffed trousers and then they entered, beneath the great arch, under the clock, and stood atop the long flight of stairs looking down, into and across the concourse of hats and shouldered seabags at the Penn Station information booth below.

"Hey! What the hell is going on?" yelled Gomez.

"This way. Follow me," answered Solly, turning his head back toward Gomez and giving absolutely no indication that anything was awry. "It's downstairs. We have to go downstairs!" Gomez was looking all about. He had lost his orientation. He was confused. He couldn't quite seem to make up his mind whether what he was experiencing was real, contrived, illusion, delusion or hallucination. He didn't know whether what he saw before him was not real and he had somehow been duped, or whether it was indeed real and somehow, in his growing paranoia, he was, at least momentarily, losing his sanity, and along with it his hold on reality. Whatever the situation he had little choice other than to do his best to keep up with Solly. And Solly was making that more difficult with every step and bound. He pushed and shoved passersby. He ran ahead as if everything he had ever known depended on his taking the lead in his little race. He weaved. He snaked.

Gomez was slowly, but unmistakably, being embraced by a sickening feeling which comprised two distinct, complementary, factors: something was indeed very wrong, and he was progressively losing his power to do anything about it. Somehow, something inside him nagged that he had been lured into a situation where he was rendered inexplicably, but most assuredly, lost. But he tried to disregard the churning in his innards, vaguely hoping that he might be able to gleen some sense, some reassuring orientation, from his surroundings at the next turn.

The next turn seemed to bring no such assurances to Gomez. Instead he actually experienced the sensation a small child might on being lost for the first time. Indeed, as he whirled around, Solly was not in sight.

Not far from where Gomez was standing, nearly wedged in place by an intensifying crowd, Solly had negotiated a quick about face. It was not so much to lose Gomez, he hadn't wanted to do that just yet, but to recheck and recover from what he thought he had just seen. For there, leaning up against the information booth, reading a copy of the **New York Herald Tribune,** was none other than Timothy. Solly was directly in front of him within moments.

"I don't believe this!" Solly spoke quietly. Timothy did not look up from his paper.

"I was wondering when you'd notice me. I saw you up there when you came in. Right on schedule. Good job...so far."

"How long have you been here?"

"Believe it or not I've only been here about three hours, myself. How do you like it? 1943, I mean." He stretched open the paper and turned the page, still not looking at Solly directly.

"I'm not sure. I haven't had much of a chance to sightsee. It's difficult to comprehend this is really '43."

"You'd better believe it. And you'd better decide what you are going to do with our friend. Because, whatever it is, he's spotted you. Here he comes."

Solly looked up in time to see Gomez shoving his way through bodies and baggage headed for other far away places enfolded deep in that year.

"Hey!" said Gomez. "Let's go! I haven't got all day!"

"I think you do, Mr. Gomez," said Solly. "You've got all day...and all year. In fact I think you've got about 45 more years to get back to where you've just been."

"What the hell are you talking about? You know, son, I think you're a lunatic. I don't know what possessed me to come with you in the first place. But I'll say this much: I'm not staying around any longer. And you're in trouble, son. Deep trouble!"

Timothy looked up from his Tribune. "Recognize me, Mr. Gomez?" Gomez was ostensibly shaken. "I recognize you. You have selfrighteous, indignant, all knowing, by the book bureaucrat written all over yourself."

"Who the hell are you?" spat out Gomez.

"I'm the guy who just set you and your lads back about 45 years. And you know, by the time you catch up, I frankly think you'll be too old to give much of a damn."

"I'll tell you something Mr..."

"Gillis. Timothy Gillis."

"I don't care what your name is. I'm going to be watching you. Both of you." He pointed his finger at Solly's face. "I know who you are, all right." Gomez turned to go as he collided with a passing sailor's seabag. It knocked his hat to the ground. He turned back at Solly and Timothy again, a bitter curl shaping his lips. "You both best be looking over your shoulders. Both of you." Then he was lost in the crushing throng. Solly heard the voice again. It was a quiet, inner voice. He did not know to whom it belonged. It just came:

'One two, one two, and through and through, the vorpal blade went snicker-snack!'

Solly picked up Gomez's hat and fingering the brim, turned to Timothy. "Are you going to tell me how you got here?" he asked, still incredulous.

"In the Rackets. I'll tell you in the Rackets when I see you." Timothy folded his paper and began making his way through the crowd in the general direction taken by Gomez. "Right now," he began raising his voice slightly, " I just want to track our friend, just for the record. I don't think he's going anywhere. But it'll make me feel better. I'll be in touch." It was the last time Solly spoke to Timothy.

A man who had had a bit too much to drink at one of the nearby BAR & GRILL accommodations poked Solly. "Shay...why aren't you in uniform?" he asked. Solly began to feel slightly out of place.

Struggling through the mob as best he could Solly succeeded in getting back up the stairs he had come down upon and through the grand arch to the outside. A woman wearing an arm band and a nurse's cap shook a can in his face and asked him to 'give to the RED CROSS'. He put a coin in the can, hoping it was a sufficiently old coin, and at least if it were not, that it would elude the hands of some curious numismatist, whom it would surely rattle. The last thing Solly saw before going into the awninged corner shop that he knew would have to be the CHEMERA bank for him, were two WACS stepping out into the sunshine, their leather handbags slung over their shoulders.

Clutching Gomez's hat, Solly thought of the two of them standing in the doorway less than an hour ago. He remembered the bills, the check Gomez was holding, his admonitions and the non-existent money machines. He tried very hard not to notice what the corner looked like at the moment. He tried with all his powers of concentration not to read the signs above the windows nor so much as glance at the merchandise in the windows. He just listened to the voice:

'He left him dead, and with his head he went galumphing back.'

And he briskly, looking straight ahead, walked inside the shop. The door did not push open as he had momentarily expected. It revolved...and became a revolving door. Solly read the 8% interest signs, saw the lucite shields before all the tellers, read the digital numerals flash the 'time elapsed on line' and felt the coolness of the 1980's warm his bones. But before he left he noticed the desks in the bank were arranged differently, most of the officers were seated, a few actually smiled as he passed, and a small sign near one officer's desk, which had not been there before, read: **'MAY WE OFFER YOU COFFEE WHILE YOU WAIT?'**

When Solly left the bank he observed the sign above the entrance read differently. **CAB**, it said, in large, bold letters. "They certainly took me for a ride," Solly muttered to himself and proceeded to hail one for himself.

"The Rackets, please, driver," Solly said, as he fished for some change.

"Beg pardon?" said the driver, one of the few old, legendary, New York cabbies left, going by his cap, craggy face, and gruff, nasal Brooklynese. "I don't think I know that one. Sorry. You hafta help me out on that one."

"Right. I meant Mortimers. Sorry. Guess I had something else on my mind."

"Right. Everybody always has something else on his mind when he gets into a cab. Right. Mortimers. I know <u>that</u> place. That's been there...forever."

MORTIMERS

The cab budged its way downtown and then wound a path deep into Greenwich Village. It was about that time, about five in the afternoon, when, according to Lewis Carroll's notion of 'Brillig', housewives (or whoever happened to be home, these days) started broiling things. And as he got out of the cab, Solly could actually smell the enticing aromas of steaks, chops and burgers. It was brillig, all right.

Mortimers, save for the delightful aromas wafting about its premises, was not so easy to distinguish. There were no lettering designations whatsoever. There was no symbol on, or above, the entryway. No mark, no emblem. There was no sign and no indication that not far beyond its old wooden door, beyond its portal's metal bars and those over Mortimers' windows, lay the warmth and comfort of good cheer and camaraderie, the refreshing taste of lusty ale, the spice of hearty food and who knew what other surprises?

The cab disappeared almost concurrently with Solly's slamming of its door and Solly was left alone, standing before the two stone steps leading up to Mortimers. He was still fingering Gomez's hat as he went inside.

Dr. Berg had said 'see you at the Rackets'. This was certainly not **THE RACKETS,** on the outside or the inside. But **THE RACKETS** <u>was</u> nowhere else. <u>This</u> was the only establishment to which Solly could turn. And, indeed, here he was.

Once inside, he climbed the few steps leading to the modest anteroom which stood before the diningroom, hovered for a moment beneath the small amber bulb which cast a yellowish glow throughout the tiny vestibule, looked down into the expanse before him and, now walking <u>down</u> another few steps, sauntered inside. There, all alone, but for his mug of ale, was Dr. Berg.

'And hast thou slain the Jabberwock? Come to my arms my beamish boy!' smiled Dr. Berg.

Solly froze at the words, but recovered quickly enough to manage an ostensibly calm approach, and, as if in answer to Dr. Berg's query, tossed Gomez's hat onto the long wooden table.

He was startled by what Dr. Berg had just uttered. It was more of the poem Solly had been hearing in his head for the past several days; nearly the end of it, just prior to the last verse. "What in the world made you say that?" asked Solly, a little pale.

"Why? It seemed a perfectly appropriate thing to say. Just short of the payoff line in **'Jabberwocky'.** In fact, I rather like the analogy myself, don't you?"

"It's just that for some inexplicable reason lines from the poem have been coursing through my mind since...well, since just before that first night at your place."

"It was probably your destiny calling. That wind blowing from your future; that future to which you are so inextricably tied. The wind takes any number of capricious forms. Language, prescient feelings, coincidences. Somehow the pieces of your puzzle may have fit all too perfectly into the pieces of Carroll's puzzle, hence the recurring lines from the poem. And my uttering of these <u>last</u> lines drew you right here to me. The parallels are clear." Dr. Berg picked up the hat. "I take it the deed is done. How did it go?"

"I'm sure you know exactly how it went. My concern now is for Timothy."

Dr. Berg's eyes dropped. He pulled a folded newspaper clipping from his vest pocket and handed it to Solly. It was from the **New York Daily Mirror,** dated September 1946. "I'm sorry to tell you this, Solly, but our friend Timothy was killed...in an automobile accident on the West Side Highway, in 1946."

His fingers shaking, Solly unfolded and began to read the yellowed and brittle clipping. He could hardly hold fast to the newspaper much less the meaning imparted by the words he saw: **'THREE MEN WERE KILLED TODAY WHEN THE 1946 PLYMOUTH THEY WERE RIDING IN FAILED TO NEGOTIATE A SHARP LEFT TURN ON MANHATTAN'S WEST SIDE HIGHWAY, AND PLUNGED ONTO THE ROCKS BELOW. DEAD WERE THE DRIVER, RAYMOND GOMEZ OF EAST 44TH STREET, N.Y., PASSENGER TIMOTHY GILLIS OF PINEHURST AVENUE, WASHINGTON HEIGHTS, N.Y., AND AN UNIDENTIFIED MAN, WHOSE ONLY RECOVERED IDENTIFICATION WAS A PLASTIC CARD CONVEYING MEMBERSHIP IN WHAT APPEARS TO BE SOME TYPE OF LIESURE CLUB. ODDLY, ALTHOUGH THE MAN'S NAME COULD NOT BE READ FROM THE CARD, WHICH WAS BADLY DAMAGED IN THE MISHAP, THE NEW YORK ADDRESS EMBOSSED ON IT DOES NOT EXIST IN THE CITY. RAIN AND SLIPPERY CONDITIONS ON THE COBBLESTONES ARE BEING BLAMED FOR THE ACCIDENT.'** Solly's eyes filled with tears and he found himself unable to speak.

"Of course we've known about this for some time," said Dr. Berg. "It was his destiny, but I suppose somehow Timothy thought he could get around it."

"I'm not altogether convinced that that is no longer a possibility."

"Perhaps. It's a pleasant notion to contemplate, circumventing the inevitable, perhaps even the Grim Reaper. But, you know, some men are very attuned to their collective unconscious, as Jung put it. They have a keen sense about where they're from, and can, at will, tap in to this vast store. Through a kind of lucid dreaming, while in a waking state, they can virtually recreate the past for themselves. And some go beyond that. They know where they're <u>going.</u> Timothy was one such man. Most of us share in this awareness. Men, like elephants who seek out their secret burial grounds shortly before death, if they take the time to communicate with themselves, know, almost exactly, when <u>their</u> time will have run out. Most, however, would rather <u>not</u> know, so they expend little effort pursuing the techniques that would lead to such vision. As we discussed before, Time has her way of bending to attract and then to entrap events. The collective unconscious is in touch with her inclinations and patterns from long ago." Dr. Berg pointed to his forhead. "It's all here. But this consciousness isn't limited to the past. Nostradamus was keenly aware of how her patterns shaped, and indeed determined, the <u>future.</u> He was able to see pretty much the whole scheme of the <u>world.</u> He foresaw events falling this way and that, because the SCHEME <u>already</u> existed. The <u>events</u> were <u>preordained,</u> according to the molds <u>already</u> set for them. These patterns that bent spacetime had long ago been shaped. Few of us have Nostradamus's gift to such a perceptive extent, but nonetheless we are all part of the mosaic and we all fall into the designs already laid out for us. But there is one hitch. Sometimes, alas, men can get cought in a kind of twist. A time warp, or worse, a maelstrom if you will, where events echo and resound until they resolve themselves and come to a kind of physical peace or inertia. It is like a very live rubber ball that has been flung or hit obliquely, with great force, against a wall in a three sided racketball court. The ball will bounce back and forth until all forces are dissipated and the sphere's final resting place is resolved."

Solly refolded and then carefully placed the newspaper clipping back on the wooden table next to Dr. Berg's ale. He made no further comment about it. "Well," he said, jauntily, "I'm going out now to enjoy this day for whatever it's worth, however it's bent. I will stroll the Village from Christopher to Carmine, from Bedford to Bleeker and Hudson to Houston. I will head uptown to the park, pass through the statues of Alice, the Mad Hatter, and the Hare consulting his pocket watch, stop a few steps away at the Conservatory Lake cake house and I will sit quietly for a moment and think of Timothy. I will watch for him there, and if I find him, we shall stroll to the Library together and have a long chat. Otherwise I will go there myself and think of the Bristol, and the reservoir, and I will always be watching for him. And now, Dr. Berg, you enjoy the day too. Perhaps we will meet again soon."

"Feel free to come by any evening. You know the way. We'll all be waiting." Dr. Berg lifted his brew.

Up the few steps, through the amber alcove, down the few steps and Solly strode out into the afternoon. He checked to see if he still had Timothy's leather notebook with him, and indeed, he had. As he flipped through it, his thumb fell upon a page filled with writing. It was a poem:

'I am old.
As old as the sun and Magellanic Clouds;
The shrouds of lingering gas
From a thousand year old supernova
Mourning the loss of that once great fiery giant.

I have known white hot reds
And blue cold ice
And a millenium slice
Of hush still dark,
Black, bereft of time.

For I am as old as...always.
I've soared on photons
Through countless realms of eons,
Back and seesaw forth
Through time and tachyons.

And I am as young as...never.
Yet to max and minimize,
Transform and metamorphosize,
And if I must,
Join cloud and dust

Awaiting ultraviolet soul
Or, hell,
Just start my own black hole.'

Timothy Gillis 1985

Solly had no doubt they would meet again, someday, somewhere. He removed the single piece of paper from the notebook and carefully placed it in his wallet. He felt good. It was going to be a clear Autumn afternoon.

'Oh frabjous day! Callooh! Callay! He chortled in his joy.'

But, somehow, Solly had seemed to have misplaced the Social Security card he normally carried in his wallet.